The Secret at Pheasant Cottage

by

PATRICIA ST. JOHN

MOODY PRESS

CHICAGO

Contents

Moody Press, a ministry of the Moody Bible Institute, is designed for education, evangelization, and edification. If we may assist you in knowing more about Christ and the Christian life, please write us without obligation: Moody Press, c/o MLM, Chicago, Illinois 60610.

Library of Congress Cataloging in Publication Data

St. John, Patricia Mary, 1920-
    The secret at Pheasant Cottage.

    SUMMARY: Raised by her grandparents, 12-year-old Lucy starts a search for her father that takes her from a prison in England to the Mediterranean coast of Spain.

    [1. Fathers and daughters—Fiction. 2. Family Life—Fiction] I. Title.

PZ7.S143Se   [Fic]   78-24384
ISBN 0-8024-7683-X

11 12 Printing/LC/Year 93 92

Printed in the United States of America

CHAPTER ONE

The Forbidden Question

LOOKING BACK NOW, I often wonder why I did not ask
questions sooner, for I was aware of some mystery sur-
rounding my life from a very early age. I think this
awareness arose from the fact that, although no one
had ever told me so, I knew quite well that I had not
always lived at Pheasant Cottage on the borders of the
Eastwood Estate. Far, far back there had been somewhere else, where skies were bluer, and a very tall man
had carried me in his arms, and I remembered perfectly well that he had once gone down on all fours
and let me ride on his back. As I grew older I used to
wonder if he could have been my father, but, strange
to say, I never asked.

I can remember, too, the first time I really began to wonder. It was eleven o'clock on a May morning. I and my friends in kindergarten were sitting and drinking milk under the apple tree in the playground. A warm breeze was blowing, tossing the pink blossom petals onto our hair, and beyond the asphalt stretched the lawn starred with daisies. Everything was perfect until Harvey Chatterley-Ffoulkes, the bank manager's son, suddenly fixed his goggle eyes on me from over the rim of his mug and asked loudly, "Lucy, why do you live with your granny? Why don't you have a proper mummy and daddy like everybody else?"

I looked around hopefully for Teacher, because I knew she would help me. But Teacher had gone to look for Jeremy, who liked to hide behind the roller towel in the cloakroom and eat lollipops, and we were all alone. All the other children were looking at me now, and I had to think of an answer quickly. I stared defiantly at Harvey and thought he looked like a fat frog, but not nearly so interesting.

"Because I don't," I replied. "Wipe your mouth, Harvey. You've got a milk moustache." This was what Granny said to me nearly every day, and so saying it usually made me feel confident and grown-up. But Harvey took no notice.

"But why not?" he insisted. "I mean, where are they? Everyone has a mummy and daddy. I mean, someone must have borned you!"

There was silence. If I said, "I don't know," they

would all laugh at me and I would cry. Every eye was turned on me. Already I could feel the tears welling up.

"Perhaps they're dead," said Mary Blossom cheerfully.

"Or p'raps they ran away and left you," breathed Janie, who read quite grown-up story books.

"Or p'raps they're divorthed," broke in Bobby, who knew all about it.

I looked around desperately and breathed a great sigh of relief, for my teacher was leading Jeremy, sticky and abashed, across the playground. Everyone's attention was diverted, and I sidled up to her, slipped my hand into hers and felt safe. But Harvey was still determined to get to the bottom of my private affairs.

"Teacher," he squeaked excitedly, "*Why* does Lucy live with her granny? I mean, why hasn't she got a daddy and—"

Teacher's clear voice cut across his question. "If I had a granny like Mrs. Ferguson, I wouldn't care if I had parents or not. She's as good as a father and mother rolled into one. You're a lucky girl, Lucy; my granny died when I was a baby. Wipe your mouth, Harvey, you've got a milk moustache. And now, everybody listen. Because it's the first of May—"

She paused dramatically, enjoying the little shiver of happy expectancy. My parentless state was completely forgotten. What wonderful event was about to take place, because it was the first of May?

"Because it's the first of May," repeated Teacher, "instead of going back to the classroom for arithmetic, we'll all go for a nature walk up to the woods on the hill and pick kingcups. They have just bloomed."

There was a shout of joy. Sixteen five-year-olds skipped, ran, or danced toward the meadow. Teacher walked behind, because she knew she would easily catch them up on the hill. I trotted quietly beside her, still holding tightly to her hand and feeling rather shaken.

I knew now that the question had been there for a long time, buried deep and never asked. Now, all of a sudden, everyone had asked it, and there was no answer. *I'll ask Granny today,* I said to myself, and then forgot all about it in the delight of the outing.

Teacher was in front now, because the hill was steep for small legs. She looked like the Pied Piper, with all her class puffing and hurrying behind her while she called back exciting instructions.

"See how many different kinds of wild flowers you can find. I said different kinds, Sally, not all dandelions. Look very quietly in the hedges; you might see a nest. Harvey, stop chattering! We want to listen to the birds, and you are frightening them all away. Now, stand still, everybody. You, too, Betsy, stop jumping up and down! Now, very quiet— Can anyone hear that thrush singing?" Then we plunged into the oak wood, and I was the first to spy a gleam of gold in the shadows and to cry out that I had seen kingcups.

Everyone broke into a charge through the undergrowth, but Teacher shooed us all back onto the path, because the year before Timothy Williams had lost a shoe in the swamp, and his mother had made a fuss. But there were plenty of flowers to be reached from the path, and presently we turned home with muddy feet and pollen-powdered noses. Teacher's shoes were the muddiest of all, from running up and down on the edge of the marsh, in her efforts to keep us from falling in it.

Parents were waiting by the schoolroom door, and one by one the children dispersed, clasping their golden bunches. But I lived farther away and dined at school, and it was four o'clock before teacher put me on the school bus. As we waited, she picked some blossom petals out of my hair and tied back my curls from my face. Then she suddenly stooped down and kissed me, and I wondered why, for she had never done such a thing before. Perhaps it had something to do with the question. Perhaps she was sorry for me.

Granny was standing at the bus stop with Shadow, our big, black Labrador, straining at his lead and barking for joy because he knew I was coming. We usually chased each other madly home, with Granny, staid and upright, walking behind. But Shadow must have been disappointed that afternoon, because I did not feel like playing. I walked quietly beside Granny, hugging my kingcups.

Then, suddenly, I asked my question. "Granny,

why do I live with you and Grandpa? Didn't I ever have a mummy and daddy? All the other children have them."

It seemed very quiet after I'd spoken. I could hear a bee buzzing in the lilac and a blackbird whistling. At last Granny answered, "Your mother was our dear daughter Alice, Lucy. She died when you were a tiny baby, and there was no one else to look after you, so Grandpa and I took you as our own little girl."

"But didn't I have a daddy?" I persisted. "And why didn't he look after me? Is he dead, too?"

And then long silence while I waited confidently for the answer, because I knew that Granny was particular about speaking the truth. "He went away," said Granny slowly, "and we never saw him again. He was not a good man, Lucy, and he could not have looked after you. You belong to us, now, and always will, just as though you were our own little girl. Look, there's Grandpa! He's seen us."

We had reached our garden, and from the way she changed the subject and pressed her lips together, I knew that I was not expected to ask any more questions. I did not mind.

Beyond the beds of massed wall-flowers and forget-me-nots the front door of our cottage stood open, and a delicious smell of baking came from the kitchen. Grandpa waved from his potato patch, his rosy face beaming a welcome. Above the chimney pots towered the feathery beech trees on the border of the Eastwood

Estate, and I knew that beneath them lay cool, shadowed pools of bluebells, foamed with cow parsley. Home was a perfect place. What did I want with a father? Let alone a bad one!

Yet somehow that old, far-away memory puzzled me, and the puzzle grew with the years. For if that tall man had been my father, then he could not have been completely bad, or he would not have held me in his arms, nor would he have gone down on all fours and let me ride on his back. But it was a riddle without an answer, and for five whole years I never mentioned it again to anyone.

CHAPTER TWO

Whitsun Camp

THOSE FIVE YEARS passed swiftly. Anyone else might have called them quite uneventful, but to me they seemed packed with excitement. I moved up into primary school and got on the under-eleven netball team, and came out top of the class in English every term. I discovered the beauty of poetry and began to scribble stories in exercise books. Grandpa had bronchitis and went to the hospital, I had measles, and the cat had kittens several times. I became a Brownie, and then a Guide, and when I was eleven years old I went to camp.

But all these interesting, and mostly pleasant, events

had nothing to do with my own real, secret life. For to me, the passing of time was not marked by terms and holidays but by the appearance of the first primrose on the stream bank, or the sheathed bud of the first wild daffodil piercing the crumbling oak leaves. Summer was the song of the first cuckoo and the unfolding of the wild roses. Autumn was the blazing colors of the leaves and the smell of bonfires. Winter was my own solitary footprints over white wastes. This was my real life, and it was so important to me that I had never much minded being an only child or not doing all the things that the other children did.

Sometimes when the girls at school laughed at me because I had never seen the sea, I would grow restless and wonder whether I would ever travel, or move beyond the familiar circle of school and home and church on Sundays. I did not see how I could, because my grandparents were growing older every year, and Grandpa, who had been head gardener at the castle on the estate for thirty years, had only a small pension. They were perfectly content to remain in their cottage, and, apart from occasional visits to relatives in Birmingham, they had no wish to take holidays. They could not, anyway, because of the poultry. And, except when my friends made fun of me, I was content, too; content to play in the woods and climb hills, to read, and to scribble stories about children who went on long journeys and traveled in ships and planes to all the golden countries I learned about in my geography book. I had my own duties in the cottage and garden, too, and the days never seemed long enough.

Sometimes Mary Blossom, my best friend, came to spend the day, and I would take her onto the estate. But Mary was a stout, practical child who preferred to arrive somewhere rather than just to wander. Her often repeated question, "Where are we going, Lucy?" annoyed me, as my unvarying reply no doubt annoyed her: "We're not going anywhere; we're just walking!" And after a time we would turn back, and skip or play games in the garden. I loved Mary dearly, but she belonged to my school world, and my woods bored her.

But from all the happy memories, one event stands out, clear and unforgettable, and that is the Whitsun Guide Camp in the Cotswolds when I was eleven years old. When Granny told Captain that I could go, provided I did not leave my undershirt off or bathe in a river with a current, I was so excited that I hardly slept for two nights. And when we actually set off in the bus with our knapsacks and bedding, I could hardly speak. I sat squeezing my clasped hands between my knees, bottling up my joy because living with elderly people had made me rather a quiet child. But gradually, as we traveled for hours through leafy lanes and sun-drenched landscapes and villages, where the houses were built of brown stone and thatch, I relaxed. We sang, we chattered, we giggled. We ate sandwiches out of plastic bags and drank lemonade out of bottles. And then we were there, high on a hill at the edge of a large, beech wood overlooking the Gloucester plain. Captain and Lieutenant were showing us where to put our tents, and how to light a fire.

That holiday came up to my highest expectations in every way. I shared a tent with Mary, and every waking hour was thrilling, from the moment we crawled out into the sweet-smelling morning to the moment we snuggled into our sleeping bags in the dark and clutched each other in mock terror when the owls hooted in the woods behind us. But I remember most vividly the early morning when I woke before anyone else, and slipping on my bathrobe and shoes I crept out into the waking world. The sun had not been up long, and a cuckoo was calling from the beeches.

Captain was wandering about in a dressing gown and saw me. "Lucy," she said, "would you like to dress and take a message to the farm for me? Straight through the wood, and climb over the fence and cross the hay-field. You'll find them milking the cows. Tell them to save us fifteen fresh eggs, and we'll fetch them later."

I was slipping on my dress when Mary's tousled head appeared out of her sleeping bag. She blinked at me. "Where are you going?" she yawned. "Shall I come too?"

"No, no," I replied hurriedly, "I shan't be long. I've got to go to the farm with a message. I've got to go now, at once. You can come and meet me if you like." I shot outside, for this was my special expedition, and

I had to go alone. The sun had reached the level of the beech boughs and was flooding the paths in the wood with radiance so bright that I could see nothing beyond. I seemed to be running into a clearing of light. Then the wood ended, and I climbed over the fence and saw the hayfield, a tangled mass of moon daisies, campions, sorrel, and buttercups all dew-covered and sparkling.

I went mad! I flung my shoes backward over the fence and leaped and danced barefoot along the path, the flowers tickling my legs. I laughed and clapped my hands, carried away with the joy of being alive on such a morning, loving the feel of the cold grass between my toes. Then, having delivered my message, I turned back and walked more slowly to prolong this beautiful, solitary hour.

But it was not to be. Mary was trotting toward me, and by the look on her round face, I knew she had a secret to tell me.

"Lucy," she began mysteriously, "do you know what?"

"What?" said I.

"Well, I came to meet you through the wood, and Captain and Lieutenant were standing by the fence."

"So what?"

"Well, they *saw* you!"

"I don't care."

"Yes, but Lucy, they talked about you. I heard them.

They didn't see me, 'cause I waited behind a tree, and I *heard* them, Lucy."

I was silent. My curiosity was thoroughly aroused, but I wasn't going to show it!

"Lucy, shall I tell you what they said about you?"

"What, then?"

"Captain said—" and here Mary's voice changed to a high, ladylike drawl—" 'Fancy good little Lucy going all wild like that! There's more in that child than meets the eye.' And Lieutenant said, 'Oh, Lucy's got plenty in her. Her teacher says her essays are brilliant. She needs to get away from those grandparents of hers occasionally, and start living.' That's what they said, Lucy. There was more, but I can't remember it all, and anyhow they turned round and saw me."

"How silly!" I replied rather crossly. "I live just as much as they do." But somehow the sparkle had gone out of the day, and all that morning while we ate breakfast and tidied and bathed in the river, I puzzled over their remarks. What was wrong with being good? And what was wrong with my grandparents? And what had I been doing all these eleven years except living? I supposed that they said it because I hadn't done all the things the others had done, and because I had never been to the sea. But after all, they knew nothing about my real life, and they had never even set foot on the Eastwood Estate. I felt rather cross and superior all day, and they must have wondered what was the matter with me. Then the delight of cooking sausages on the campfire drove the whole thing out of my mind.

But it had stirred up all the old questions. I was different.

That night I lay awake for a long time, with Mary snoring beside me, and listened to the owls and the rustle of the beech leaves. I tried to remember the face of the tall man who had gone down on all fours. But it was no good. It had gone forever.

CHAPTER THREE

The Letter in the Drawer

CAMP WAS OVER, but time sped on so fast that I seldom looked backward or forward but just enjoyed each new day. Once again summer blazed into autumn, and I moved up into secondary school.

Once again the snow fell and blanketed the hills. Again I collected pinecones and roasted chestnuts and made secret Christmas presents. Again I heard the bleat of the first lamb at twilight, smelled the warm south wind stirring the buds, and knew that spring was on the way.

And then it was the last day of the Easter term and the world was a singing chorus of green and gold and blossom. Regular lessons were over, and everyone was

19

fidgety and longing for the holidays. Miss Bird, our English teacher, was reading us a poem, but the window was wide open; we could hear the ringdoves cooing, and the sheep calling their lambs. Miss Bird was getting little attention.

She closed the book, stepped to the blackboard and wrote "SUMMER HOLIDAY" in large letters. There was a slight stir of interest. A few heads lifted.

I thought Miss Bird looked like summer itself, standing there in her yellow pullover in a pool of sunshine. "You will be planning your summer holidays soon," she announced, "so this is a competition for you to try. Next term there will be a prize for the best entry. You can write a story, or tell about what you did last year or what you plan to do this year. Anything you like, but try to get the feeling of summer into it."

She looked around at our blank faces. "The feeling of summer seems to be rather a sleepy one," she said with a smile. "Let's collect some ideas and write them on the board. Mary, when I say "summer holiday," what do you think of?"

Mary jerked to attention. "Er—" she began. "Er—hot—and—ice cream—"

"Yes, all right. Somebody else? Jennifer?"

"Bathing—the beach—donkeys—"

"Punch and Judy show—bingo—"

"Tennis."

"Camping in our caravan."

"Riding my pony."

Miss Bird was writing rapidly. She turned and faced the thoroughly awakened class.

"Yes, that's right, but what about the places you go to? Anna, where did you go for your last summer holiday?"

"We toured Scotland in our car."

"And what was Scotland like in the summer?"

"Oh, mountains and lakes, and it rained, and the car broke down. We saw some castles and battlefields and things, and we watched for the Loch Ness Monster all one day, but no luck!"

Miss Bird gave a small sigh and looked at me.

"Lucy?" she asked.

Somebody gave a little titter, and Mary Blossom sprang to my rescue. "Lucy never goes away," she explained. "Her grandparents can't take holidays because—"

"That will do, Mary," interrupted Miss Bird. "Summer is here at home, too, not just in the holiday places. Besides Lucy did go on holiday. She went to the Whitsun Camp. Can you tell us about summer in the Cotswolds, Lucy?"

I closed my lips tightly and scowled at my teacher. Why should she ask me? She knew I never went anywhere. Then I glanced at her face and realized she was not making fun of me at all. She really wanted my help. She and I felt the same about summer, and she was appealing to me. I stared out of the window and tried to remember. Summer on the Cotswolds!

"The smell of honeysuckle and new-mown hay," I began slowly, "and that sort of shiny light coming through the beech leaves at sunset so all the leaves separate. Seeing stars through a hole in the canvas— and the dew all sparkly on the flowers in the early morning. And bathing in the river. Kingfishers came out of a hole in the bank and we swung on the willow branches." Memories were flooding up, and I could have gone on forever. Then I suddenly noticed the astonished faces of the other girls gaping at me, and I blushed and stopped short. Miss Bird had her back to us, and I had never seen her write so fast before. The silence was broken by the bell and a joyful clatter of desk lids. It was time for break.

"You really did save the situation," said Mary admiringly as we drank our milk. "I just couldn't think of anything but ice cream. I can't think how you manage to be so poetical, Lucy! I should think you'd get the prize easily."

I doubted it, for how could my Cotswold experiences compare with touring Scotland in a car, or even going to the sea? I felt restless as I wandered home from the bus stop that afternoon. I had recently been studying a poem called *The Forsaken Merman*, all about the sea. I wished I could see the sea!

Now the great tides shoreward flow,
Now the wild, white horses play,
Champ and chafe and toss in the spray. . . .

What did they look like, I wondered, and where did they come from, those great tides? I felt a strange stirring at the heart of me, a reaching out for change. I opened the gate and walked up the garden path, so absorbed in my thoughts, that I failed to call out my usual greeting. I stepped quietly into the passage. I was about to enter the doorway of the room where my grandparents were sitting with their backs to me, and I could not help hearing what they said. And having heard, my heart seemed to miss a beat, and I stood as though turned to stone.

"But Elsie," said my grandfather gently, "she will *have* to know soon. She is twelve years old, and after all, he is her father."

"But not yet, not yet," cried my grandmother. "There are still almost two years to go. Anything may happen in two years."

I stepped back very softly and crept out through the front door. They must not know that I had heard. I wanted to run away and hide in the wood and think and think, but Shadow spied me from the kitchen and came charging to meet me, slobbering on my feet, wagging his tail, and jumping up to kiss me. There was nothing to do but to step back inside, just in time to see Granny fold a letter and slip it into the top drawer of her bureau.

But they greeted me as usual, and I helped to get high tea. The sun streamed in at the west window through a lattice of larch boughs and made patterns on the wall. It should have been a happy, chatty tea as we caught up on the news of the day, but somehow we were all strangely silent. It seemed as though some shadow had come between us, and I was almost glad when the meal was over.

"Any homework tonight?" asked Granny.

"No, Granny," I answered. "Tomorrow's the last day of term, so we don't do proper lessons. Can I go out for a bit when we've washed up?"

She looked at me with a strangely tender expression. "Grandpa and I will see to the washing up tonight, love," she answered. "You run along, now, with Shadow. It's a beautiful evening. But come back before sunset."

Grandpa walked to the gate with me and asked where I was going, but I just pointed vaguely up the hill. I wanted to get away by myself, and I sped up the steep slope to the left of the house and flung myself into an old grassy trench where the ancient Britons were said to have made a last stand against the Romans. Shadow came and rested his nose against my arm. Within reach of my hand, small bracken fronds were unfolding like babies' fingers, and in front of me, over the rim of the trench, lay the great plain, bathed in the last light. Every road was lit up by the sunset and seemed to run purposefully into the horizon. Every river was a shining ribbon. It all looked like a bright, clear map, and I suddenly realized what a vast place the world was. So many roads leading away from the safe shelter of my little home—such far, far distances!

What was I to do? If I asked, they would probably not tell me; and anyhow, they didn't want me to ask. But I had to know, because he was my father, and I was his daughter, Lucy. Besides, I was twelve years old, old enough to be trusted. Even Grandpa recognized that, but Granny always had the last word, so that didn't help. Then as I lay there, chewing a bracken shoot and watching the sun sink toward the far Welsh mountains, an idea came to me—an idea so wicked that I gasped and felt my face flush crimson.

I would stay awake until my grandparents were asleep, and then I would creep down, find the letter in the drawer, and read it. I would see the address and find out where my father was and what it was all about. Of course, I knew perfectly well what Granny thought about people who eavesdropped and looked at letters that didn't belong to them, but I decided it just couldn't be helped. *After all,* I argued with myself, *this letter, in a sense, does belong to me, because it's from my father.* Then I realized that the sun was sinking below the rim of the world, and I jumped up and raced down across the slippery grass, scattering the sheep in all directions. Grandpa was at the gate, peering short-sightedly down the road.

Evenings at the cottage were cozy times. We sat around the fire in winter, but on warm spring evenings we sat by the open window, and I knitted or stuck in my stamps, while Granny read aloud—mostly from the shabby old books she had loved as a child: *Jackanapes, The Secret Garden, Heidi* and *John Halifax Gentleman*. At this time we were halfway through *David Copperfield,* and Dora and Steerforth and the Pegotty family had become part of my life. I could hardly wait from evening to evening to hear the next installment.

But tonight I did not want to sit quietly with my grandparents in the soft circle of light, as though there were nothing the matter, and even little Em'ly's troubles seemed small and unimportant in comparison with my own. I felt outside the circle, a deceiver, and the loneliness of it was almost more than I could bear. To their great surprise and disappointment, I pretended to be sleepy and crept miserably up to my bedroom.

CHAPTER FOUR

The Truth Comes Out

How was I going to stay awake? This was my big problem. If I could have stayed dressed, it would have been easier. But I had to get into bed, because Granny always came to say good night to me and to make sure that I had folded my clothes properly and said my prayers. I always said my prayers, either "Our Father" or the old baby one Granny had taught me when I was four, "Jesus, tender Shepherd, hear me," and they took about twenty seconds each. The saying of them had become such a habit that they meant nothing to me at all.

But tonight, as I ducked down on my knees, something seemed wrong. For the first time I really thought about what I was saying. Could I say, "Forgive us our trespasses," when I was just about to trespass on Granny's private correspondence?

I switched over to "Jesus, tender Shepherd," but it was no better. "Let my sins be all forgiven; bless the friends I love so well."

I gave up and jumped into bed, and a moment later Granny appeared. But she did not glance at my folded clothes or mention my prayers. She put her hand on my forehead and asked if I felt all right.

"Yes, thank you," I answered.

"Are you sure, Lucy?" She lingered, as though loath to leave me. "Have you a headache? How about a drink of hot chocolate?"

This was supposed to be a big treat, but my stomach seemed tied in knots, so I just smiled, and shook my head and closed my eyes. She went away slowly and I knew she was watching me from the door. But at last I heard her footsteps going downstairs, and then I sat up and looked around.

Perhaps an exciting adventure story would help keep me awake. I dared not switch on the light, but I had a flashlight, and by its light I tiptoed to my bookcase. I turned the pages of one book after another, but nothing seemed exciting except the letter in the bureau, and all adventure seemed tame compared with the adventure of creeping downstairs and solving the mystery of my own life.

I sat down by the open window and leaned my arms on the sill. The scent of growing things rose like incense in the warm dark—spring shoots growing upright, closed to darkness and open to light—and my heart ached. A screen of larch trees sheltered us from the windy hills, and the night seemed to throw a mantle round our safe, little home and Granny, Grandpa and me, so secure and happy till now. Why did this mysterious shadow have to come between us and spoil everything? I nearly decided to forget about that letter and cuddle down, yield to sleep — but no! I *must* find out, and this was probably my last chance. I leaned against the wall and dozed a little. Then I woke with a start, for my grandparents were coming upstairs.

I dived into bed, and, as I had anticipated, Granny came in and stood over me, with a flashlight in her hand.

"She's asleep, all right," I heard her whisper, "but mark my words, Herbert, there's something the matter with the child."

I could hear Grandpa's distressed murmur and the click of their door shutting. Another eternity, when I staggered up and down in my room, swaying with sleep, and then the line of light under their door disappeared. In another ten minutes or so I listened at the keyhole and could hear Granny's steady snoring, and knew that my time had come.

I tiptoed downstairs and boldly switched on the light in the sitting room. I was shivering with guilty excitement as I pulled open the drawer. The letter I wanted was not lying on the top. Granny must have hidden it, and I had no idea what it looked like, so I thumbed through the pile, glancing at the addresses. They were mostly bills or letters from Granny's sister in Birmingham or Grandpa's nephew in Stockton-on-Tees. Nothing mysterious until I had nearly reached the bottom of the bundle—and there was an unusual sort of letter with the address printed at the top, "Her Majesty's Prison, Greening."

I stood frozen, rooted to the spot, staring at the address, and only after a long time did my eyes move down to the actual letter. "Dear Mr. and Mrs. Ferguson," it began. "As the time of my imprisonment will soon be drawing to a close, I am writing to you on the subject of the guardianship of my daughter, Lucy. I am very grateful. . . ."

I was so absorbed by what I was reading that I had ceased to notice anything, even the footsteps on the stairs and the opening of the door. It was only when he was right in front of me that I became aware of Grandpa and realized that I was caught in the act. I thrust the letter behind my back and burst into frightened, defiant tears.

"Lucy, Lucy, my dear child, whatever is the matter?" whispered Grandpa, shutting the door very cautiously, as though we were hatching a plot together. I gulped and looked at him pleadingly, and I suddenly realized that there was nothing to be afraid of. This was no policeman catching a criminal red-handed, but a distressed little old man in a very shabby dressing gown, who couldn't even see what I was doing because he'd left his spectacles upstairs. He peered at me shortsightedly and drew me to the sofa.

"You're shivering, child," he said. "I'm going up to your room to get a blanket. Put on the kettle, my dear, and let's have a cup of tea."

A cup of tea was Grandpa's cure for all ills.

He came tiptoeing down in a few minutes and wrapped me up warmly. I stopped shivering and hiccuping and relaxed. I could see that he was very anxious not to wake Granny, and not until we were both sipping cups of tea did he remember to ask me what I was doing.

He had not noticed the letter at all. He had merely seen the light shining from the window and crept downstairs to turn it out. But my secret was too heavy and shocking to carry alone any longer. I needed Grandpa's help, and I leaned against him and told him all about it.

"You see, Grandpa, I know it's wrong to read other people's letters, but I had to know, hadn't I? He's my father, and I'd always wondered, only Granny would never tell me."

"No, it wasn't right," said Grandpa, "And I'm glad I came. But maybe we should have told you sooner, or maybe you should have asked us again, instead of trying to find out alone. But in any case, it's high time you knew, although there is nothing to be afraid of. There is still quite a long time to go, if he does the whole sentence, and by that time you'll be nearly fourteen, and you'll be allowed to choose for yourself. I don't reckon any court of law would force you to go with your father against your will. We can't stop his seeing you, but he can visit you here."

"But does he want me?" I asked. "I only saw the beginning of the letter."

"Well, now, yes, he seems to want you," replied Grandpa gently taking the letter out of my hand. "But we've consulted lawyers, Lucy, and he couldn't take you from here unless you wanted to go, which of course you wouldn't. He wouldn't be anything of a guardian for you. In fact I'm afraid he's a very bad man."

"What did he do?" I asked. "Was I there?"

"Yes," said Grandpa, and he spoke very sadly. "It all happened after you were born, and after our dear, dear Alice died. She met him at a friend's house, and he courted her. But your Grandmother, she felt it wasn't right, and she wouldn't agree to their engagement, not at any price. He was an unsettled kind of chap, so they just ran away and got married on their own. They went to Spain. He had a guest house there, or some such thing, and we never saw our daughter again. She died when you were born."

Grandpa's voice trailed off sorrowfully, and he seemed to have forgotten about me. I gave his arm a small shake.

"I'm sorry, Grandpa," I whispered. "But what happened next? I mean, what happened to me?"

"We begged him to send you home to us, but he never so much as answered our letters. I believe he loved your mother very much and was heartbroken when she died. The second time we wrote, it was sent back to us. He had left that address and no one rightly knew where he'd gone."

"But where was I, Grandpa? Did he take me with him?"

"Oh, yes, but we don't know much about the next three years. I believe he drank a good deal, and got in with some drug business, helping to convey drugs up through Spain into France. Then he came back to England, and the police were waiting for him. It was all in the papers, but to tell you the truth, Lucy, I didn't rightly understand it. It was about that time that he brought you to us."

"Oh! So you've seen him?"

"Oh, yes. He arrived in a taxi, all unexpected like, with you in his arms, and asked us to look after you for a spell. I think he knew he was about to be jailed, but he didn't tell us so at the time. We had never seen him before, but there was no mistaking you. Such a funny little mite you were, and the image of your dear mother—the same thick, curly hair, the same grey eyes."

"But my father, Grandpa! Did he love me?"

"Oh, yes; there was no doubt about that. You'd been well cared for, too, and you talked a sort of mixture of English and Spanish. He said you'd had a Spanish nurse. He wouldn't stay or tell us much. He just put you into Granny's arms. You clung to him and cried at first, but then you fell asleep. And when you woke up next morning, you might have belonged to us all your life. You were just three and a half."

"But tell me about my father, Grandpa. Didn't he ever come back?"

"No; a few days later it was all in the papers, and he wrote telling us he'd got a ten-year sentence and asking us to care for you. Your Granny wasn't surprised—said she'd known he was a bad lot from the beginning, and we must make sure as you were never told. But when he comes out you'll have to know, Lucy, and maybe 'tis best you know now. But I sometimes wish, that for Alice's sake we'd done differently."

"What was she like, Grandpa? My mother, I mean."

"She took after your Granny, my dear. Your Granny was the village school mistress when I married her, and there were many as said that she married beneath her. They were right, for I never had much book learning, but she seemed satisfied. We weren't over young and we only had but Alice, and she was the living spit of your Granny—only more so, in a way. Your Granny always loved reading, but Alice, she had a passion for books and learning. She'd dance round the garden saying poetry to herself and lie there under the rowan tree in summer, scribbling away. We managed to send her to college, too. She got degrees and all the rest of it, but she couldn't abide to be long away from the cottage and the hills. She was always coming back— until she met him. You're very like her, Lucy, and we don't want—"

"Herbert, what in the name of heaven are you doing down there?" Granny suddenly called in a loud whisper from the top of the stairs, and we both jumped guiltily to our feet and thrust our teacups into an inconspicuous corner. "I'm coming, Elsie," called Grandpa, but I seized his arm.

"Are you going to tell her?" I faltered.

"Oh, yes, of course," murmured Grandpa, hurrying to the door, and I realized that he had never had a secret from her in his life and would not know how. I kept tight hold of his arm as we climbed the staircase.

"And *may* I ask what Lucy is doing?" Granny bristling with indignation, looked rather fierce and unfamiliar in her hair curlers. "*Is* there any reason?"

"Yes dear, there is. I'll tell you all about it. Lucy, go back to bed." And to my great astonishment, I saw Granny propelled speechless into the bedroom, and the door was slammed on me.

I climbed into bed, shivering, but it was a long, long time before I went to sleep. Wonder, shock, excitement, regret, and a strange, cold fear of the future kept me awake. One day this bad man was going to reappear, and I was going to have to know what to do. I tossed and turned until a cock crowed far away and some sheep bleated up on the hill. A bird trilled the first few notes of the dawn chorus, and though the stars still blazed, another spring morning had begun.

I was suddenly drowsy, and the confusion of my

thoughts quieted. I just saw a man, heartbroken, because his wife had died, kissing his baby daughter good-bye for ten years and sitting in a dark, lonely dungeon (for that was what the word *prison* conveyed to me). And I had never known. Perhaps I could have comforted him, even if he was such a bad man. I buried my face in my arms and wept, and the next thing of which I was conscious was the sun streaming into my bedroom, and Granny standing by my bed with a cup of tea.

"Wake up, Lucy," she said. "I let you sleep on. But you'll have to hurry to catch the bus."

But there was no afternoon school, and as soon as we had washed up the dinner things, Granny and I settled down in the garden, and I heard exactly what Granny thought about children who sneaked downstairs at night to read other people's letters, and said they were sleepy when they were not. By the time she had finished, we had rather lost sight of the main issue; and I felt too crushed and ashamed of myself to ask any of the questions I wanted to ask.

"Sorry, Granny," I said, because that was what she expected me to say. And then I quite surprised myself by adding, "But I had to know sometime, didn't I, Granny? After all, he is my father, and I am twelve years old."

She stared at me, but the sharp answer I expected never came. "Lucy" she said, and to my amazement her voice trembled. "I hope you will never have to have anything to do with him. No one could take you away from us now—not after all these years."

I stared back and saw that her eyes were full of fear—fear because she loved me, and because the shadow of losing me had hung over her, day and night, for eight years. I flung my arms around her neck and hugged her. Then I ran off into the wood, with Shadow at my heels.

It was quiet in the wood, and now that the first shock of discovery was over, I wanted to think. Strange new thoughts were surging up inside me. I ran through the wood anemones and primroses to the edge of the trees where a sleepy stream ambled along, its golden water lingering round small rocks. All over the bank, wild daffodils pierced the dead oak leaves, and catkins pranced above me, scattering pollen on my hair. Here I sat, resting my chin on my knees, and realized I had changed. Over the last twenty-four hours I had begun to grow up in a hurry.

Granny was a very just woman. She always listened to what I had to say, and when she scolded me I usually knew in my heart that what she said was right. But today I was not so sure. I felt less ashamed of my "creeping and peeping," as she called it, than I had expected to, because it seemed to me that the letter hadn't really belonged to Granny at all. My father was mine, and the news belonged to me, and it was up to me alone to decide what I was going to do about it.

CHAPTER FIVE

Don

IT WAS WARM and peaceful where I sat. No sound but
the gurgle of a brook in no hurry to move and the
muted excitement of nesting birds in the wood behind
me. Then suddenly Shadow lifted his head and
growled, and I turned to see a boy limping along the
bank—a pleasant-looking boy of about my own age,
with thick brown hair and green-hazel eyes rather far
apart in his heart-shaped face.

"Hi!" said the boy unceremoniously. "Do you happen to have a handkerchief?"

I fished up the sleeve of my pullover and brought
out a rather grubby one. He sat down beside me and
held out his foot. It was badly cut and bleeding freely.

"Go down to the stream and hold it in cold water first," I said, remembering my Guides' first aid course, and he obeyed, sitting on a stump and dangling his foot in the water. Then I tied it tightly with my handkerchief and we sat watching whether the blood would seep through or not. I had had little to do with boys since I left primary school, and I was usually shy of them, but a boy in distress was different.

"How did you do it?" I asked.

"I trod on some broken glass in the stream back there. I was paddling."

"But you're not supposed to be in the stream at all. This is a pheasant preserve, and it's a private estate."

He smiled engagingly. "Then what are you doing here?" he asked.

"Oh, I belong here," I replied grandly. "My grandfather was head gardener at the castle for thirty years. They always send him several brace of pheasant when they shoot."

"Really?" replied the boy. "But isn't it rather boring playing in this great place all alone? I mean, wouldn't it be more fun if there were someone else?"

I had never really thought about it.

"Well, yes," I replied slowly, "I suppose it would, within reason. Do you often come here?"

"This is my first time. We've only just come to live around here. I didn't come in through the gate. I came from the valley and I got under the barbed wire at the back. I belong to a natural history society at

School, and I'm doing a project on wildlife in this county. These woods are the best place to watch, and I'm very careful about pheasants. I want to dam the stream lower down, to make a pool. Then more animals would come there to drink; especially early in the morning. Oh! Look at my foot!"

The handkerchief was saturated with blood. Something had to be done at once.

"Where do you live?" I asked.

"Down in Eastbury. But I couldn't walk as far as that. I might bleed to death!"

"Well, come up to my house, and Granny will bandage it and phone for a taxi. We live by the main gate. It's only about ten minutes' walk."

"Won't she mind? I'm a trespasser, remember."

"Oh, no! She's not interested in pheasants. Grandpa is, but he's out in the greenhouse, and he's so interested in his tomatoes that he won't think to ask what you're doing. Come on!"

It took us nearly twenty minutes to reach the house, because the injured foot was very painful. Fortunately he had a knife, and we cut a stout thorn stick for him to lean on. He limped bravely along, and as we walked, we talked, and I learned quite a lot about him.

His name was Donald, but he said I might call him Don, and he was twelve years old. His father had taken over the Royal Midland Hotel just before Christmas and was making a good thing of it. He was obviously tremendously proud of his father. He hadn't any brothers and sisters and he went to boarding school, so he hadn't made any friends in the town yet.

We had nearly reached home when he turned to me and said, "And what about you?" What were you doing all by yourself?"

"Oh, just thinking."

"Thinking? D'you often just sit and think? What do you think about?"

"Oh, nothing much. Here we are; this is our house."

"What a fantastic garden! D'you live with your grandparents?"

"Yes."

He stood for a moment, taking in the great drifts of daffodils in the grass and the almond tree, heavy with blossom, and I knew that he admired our cottage as much as I did. When he spoke again, it was almost wonderingly.

"Do you live here always? Where are your parents?"

"I haven't—well, I haven't really got any. My mother died. That's what I was thinking about. Look, there's Grandpa working on the rockery, and Granny bringing in the washing. Granny, I've brought a boy. He's hurt his foot."

Granny hurried across the lawn, brimming over with kindness and concern. In no time at all, Donald was sitting on a stool and soaking his foot in the bathroom, and Granny was bustling around organizing us all.

"I think that should be stitched," she said, surveying the ugly cut. "Can we phone your father, and can he fetch you? If so, Grandpa can go along to the phone booth. Lucy, make a cup of tea, there's a good girl!"

"Oh, yes, Dad's at home, and we've got a car," said Don, who had stopped bleeding to death. "I'll write down the number. Tell him where I am, by the big iron gates of the estate. I'll be sitting on the garden wall waiting for him."

So Grandpa trotted off, and Granny bound up the cut, and I made tea in the sunny kitchen, because Don wasn't really a parlour visitor. He soon hobbled downstairs and drank a mug of tea and wolfed two pieces of Granny's chocolate sponge cake in a great hurry, because he didn't want to miss his father. Then we went out to wait on the wall in the evening sunshine.

"Thanks a lot, Lucy," he said. "I really would have been in the soup without you and your Gran. And they didn't say anything about the trespassing, either."

"'Tisn't them," I replied, "it's the gamekeepers. They can be really nasty. But I was thinking. Suppose I took you in—"

"If I said I was a friend of yours, they'd let me come, wouldn't they?" broke in Don eagerly. "I do want to dam that stream and make a big pool. How about helping me, Lucy? When my foot's better. Oh! Here's my dad!"

A car drew up sharply. The driver gave a friendly hoot and jumped out.

"What on earth, Don?" he began. "Can you walk? Where's the kind lady who rescued you?"

Granny came to the gate and said it was a pleasure, but the foot ought to be stitched. And Don stood grinning from ear to ear, delighted with his adventure and his dad. Grandpa joined us with a bunch of daffodils and early narcissi, and we parted on the best of terms.

"Bye, Lucy," called Don, hobbling to the car. "I'll be seeing you!" And a few moments later they were off, and I watched his waving hand until it disappeared around the corner. Then I walked slowly back to the house. Granny stood in the doorway looking very pleased with herself.

"Lucy," she said, "I phoned Miss Bird this afternoon. I thought you might like to get away for a little holiday over Easter. She says she can fit you into a Guide camp in Derbyshire for a week. Would you like that?"

I stared at her blankly. If she had said this to me yesterday, I would have gone crazy with excitement. But now—if I went away to camp, I would never dam the stream or watch for squirrels in the early morning with Don. And if I wasn't there, he would never be able to say he was my friend.

"I don't know, Granny," I answered slowly. "It's not as if they were girls from our school, is it? It was different sharing a tent with Mary. I wouldn't know any of these girls, would I?"

"I guess you'd know them pretty well by the end of the week," retorted Granny, "but it's as you like. We don't want to get rid of you, do we Grandpa? I just thought the holidays were kind of lonesome for you here, but maybe you can ask your friends up."

"I'm not lonely, Granny," I answered quietly. "I'd rather stay for Easter. It's fun here at Easter, and I— well, I just don't want to go away."

So I stayed and waited to see what would happen next, and four or five days later Don reappeared on a bicycle with his foot well bandaged. I had been to town with Granny on the bus, and we were all having tea when he turned up, so he came in and joined us. He got on very well with my grandparents. He had never had any, he explained, because his dad had been an orphan and his mother had come from South Africa, and he seemed to take it for granted that he could share mine. He ate a great deal and then suggested we go to look at the stream.

It was the first of several happy mornings and evenings. They were the best time to watch wildlife, he said, and anyhow, he had a job working for his dad during the day. He was saving up for a new bike. He was always anxious to get back by 9 A.M. and seemed to think the hotel might collapse if he were late. But we dug out a pool big enough to wade in from the stream bed, and dammed it.

I would often hear his bicycle bell soon after sunrise. I would dress and creep down, explaining to a sorrowful Shadow that he could not come, and then I would run out into the light and blossom and birdsong to join Don crouching in the bushes to watch birds, squirrels, and rabbits. And once on a never-to-be-forgotten early morning, when we were climbing a tree and not watching at all, we suddenly saw a vixen playing with her three roly-poly cubs. They tried to bite her tail, but she cuffed them onto their backs, where they lay, waving their little paws in the air, and rolling over each other. At last they grew tired, and the mother lay on her side and let them suck, while we sat motionless, watching from above, until the meal was over and the vixen trotted away through the daffodils, her babies trotting unsteadily behind her.

Our talk was seldom personal. He told me about birds and foxes and fossils and what his dad said and did, and I told him about the Forsaken Merman and the Highwayman and David and Emily, and Tommy Traddles. It was halfway through the holidays before Don asked the question I dreaded, the question which always came up in the end and which I had never been able to answer. Now that I could answer, it was almost worse.

We were wandering home on a quiet, gray April evening, noticing things, as was our way. I had stopped to look at the leaf fingers released from the horse-chestnut buds, and he was peering around through a pair of binoculars which his dad had given him for his birthday. I wished I had given him a birthday present, but I hadn't known about it.

"I can see that thrush right up close," he exulted. "I can almost count the speckles on her breast. Dad knew I wanted binoculars, and he bought me a really good pair. Lucy, what happened to your Dad? Did he die, too?"

Suddenly I realized that I no longer dreaded this question. I wanted to share my tangled thoughts with someone to whom I could speak quite freely, without fear of hurting their feelings. "Sit down on this log, Don," I said, "And I'll tell you all about it."

I told him everything, all about my past, and the letter, and creeping downstairs, all about Granny and Grandpa and their fears, all about the great big question that kept me awake at night: when he comes, what shall I do? "What would you do, Don, if your dad were a wicked man in prison and yet he wanted you?"

And Don, tossing his thick, brown hair back from his forehead, replied without hesitation, "I would find him somehow, somewhere, and I would say to him, 'I don't care what you've done, Dad; I'm still your boy!'"

CHAPTER SIX

Dance of the Badgers

WE WENT HOME, and Don, after begging a bun and a cup of tea off Granny, cycled away into the dusk as usual. But once again, something had happened. Somehow, through that single sentence of Don's, I suddenly knew what to do. All my confused sense of right and wrong, my conflicting loyalties, seemed to have come to rest on that single sentence, as though it were a compass that was pointing me home. Somehow I must find my father, or wait until he found me, and tell him that whatever he had done, I was still his girl. For the first time, I felt I was starting out in the right direction instead of running around in circles. For the first time since the reading of that letter, I fell asleep the moment my head touched the pillow.

47

Two days later it was Good Friday, and Granny, Grandpa, and I went to the service in the little Norman priory that nestled against the fall of the hill like an old gray rock washed by bright seas of daffodils. I quite liked going to church; I liked wearing my best clothes and singing hymns, and I loved the musty smell and the simple beauty of the arches and pillars. During the sermon I usually made up stories while Grandpa snoozed and Granny listened.

That day, though, it was a different sort of service. There was no sermon, just hymns and prayers, and I found myself listening, really listening. Then we sang a hymn I had known since I was small, and I found myself thinking, really thinking, about the words: "He died that we might be forgiven, He died to make us good."

If that was true and bad people could change and be forgiven, it might make all the difference to my father. While I was still thinking this out, the service ended, and we streamed out of the cool, cavelike priory into the green and gold of the April morning. I wondered what it was like to come out of prison, to be forgiven. I walked home very quietly, still thinking hard.

That afternoon I joined Grandpa, who was thinning out seedlings, and weeded the bed beside him. I felt I needed to extract every ounce of information that I could from him, and besides, I liked talking to Grandpa.

"Did my mother like gardening, Grandpa?" I began conversationally.

"Well, now, I don't know that she did much. She loved wild, growing things, and wandering about, but she liked reading better than working in gardens. She was a great one for book learning, was Alice."

"And I'm really like her, Grandpa?"

He smiled very tenderly. "You might be her all over again, pretending to do a bit of weeding and sitting back and talking instead. That was her way! It was, 'Dad this,' and, 'Dad that'! I never got any work done when she was about."

"But aren't I like my father, Grandpa? Surely you can't be like only one parent?"

His smile faded. "I don't think you favor him at all, Lucy, and even if you did—" he paused, groping for words. "It's like this, or so it seems to me: if you cross a weak strain with a healthy strain, and then you take the seedlings and dung them and water them and shelter them and keep the slugs off 'em—well, they'll grow up healthy plants. The weak strain'll die out. We've tried to give you plenty of sunshine and shelter, Lucy."

"And you've kept the slugs off me," I added with a giggle. "But Grandpa, don't bad people ever turn good? I mean, don't people ever change?"

Grandpa considered this for a long time.

"Well," he said at last, leaning on his spade, "even

the Bible says something about not gathering grapes from thistles. Flowers is flowers and weeds is weeds, but people *can* change, by the grace of God. But prison's a poor soil, Lucy! They mostly come out worse than they went in! But there *is* the grace of God. You'd best ask your granny about it."

He gave a deep sigh and stooped to his seedlings, and I sighed too and grubbed up a few more weeds, for Grandpa's answer had given me little hope or comfort. Then I glanced up and noticed a heap of manure beside the toolshed and gave a little cry of pleasure. Two white narcissi appeared to be springing out of it, although whether their bulbs were embedded in the dirt, or whether their spearlike sheaths had pierced it, I could not tell. *Such beautiful flowers out of such dirty, smelly manure!* I said to myself. *It's like the grace of God. Ugly things* can *turn beautiful. I think bad people* can *become good.*

I saw little of Don until after Easter, for he had been very busy helping his father, and the new bike was in view. He had earned quite a lot of money taking luggage up in the elevator, working in the garden, cleaning the car, and running errands for Mr. Smith.

"Who is Mr. Smith?" I inquired idly. It was a warm, sleepy afternoon, and we sat dangling our feet in the pool, eating our tea and exchanging news. The daffodils were nearly over, but a faint impression of blue in the shadows heralded the arrival of the bluebells.

Mr. Smith, explained Don with his mouth full, was

their one and only resident lodger. He had taken an attic about ten days previously and was going to stay until the summer. He was a nice man who had traveled in lots of countries. He had been in an avalanche and seen a bullfight, but he wasn't very strong and he had a bad cough. Don liked talking to him but wasn't allowed to disturb him much because he was always busy.

"What does he do?" I asked.

"He writes books," replied Don casually. He's got a whole shelf of them, but he won't let me read them. He says—"

"Writes books!" I gasped. "Do you mean to say he writes real books—to be printed, and people read them?"

"Of course! What else would you do with books? Eat 'em?"

I gazed at him in reverent wonder. He ran errands for a real, live author, whose books were printed! I thought of the exercise books in my bedroom, filled with pages of happy scribble. But would I ever write anything that could be printed? And who would tell me how to set about it? "I should like to meet Mr. Smith," I said boldly.

"Actually," replied Don, "he'd like to meet you. I told him how you wrote stories and poems and things, and he said he was interested in children who wrote things, and he'd like to see some of your pieces. Perhaps he'll come up to the woods with me one day when he's better, but I shan't be coming for a few days. Dad thinks there's some badgers in a little wood off the Tewkesbury Road, and we're going to watch. They come out when it's getting dark."

"Wish I could see them," I said.

"OK," said Don good-naturedly, "but you can't come until I know they exist. If they are really there, we'll try and fix something. Badgers are worth seeing."

He was as good as his word. He came peddling up the hill, very breathless and excited, about five days later, and burst into the kitchen where Granny and I were spending a peaceful afternoon baking for the church fête.

"Please, Mrs. Ferguson," he announced, "can Lucy come? Mum says she can have high tea with us at home, and then she can come and see the badgers. We saw hundreds of them, Mrs. Ferguson! Well, I mean, we saw at least seven! It was pitch dark, and we watched them dancing and boxing."

"May I ask how, in the pitch dark?" asked Granny dryly.

"Well, it got pitch dark as we watched," explained Don, "and it was pitch dark coming home in the car. When we first saw them it was sunset. The sky was all red, and we lay for ages waiting for them to come. You have to keep very, very still, Lucy. You mustn't move for about an hour."

"That must be quite a trial for you!" remarked

Granny, observing the gyrating Don. "And who is going with you? Your father will take you, and bring Lucy back, will he?"

Don shook his head. "Dad's busy tonight," he explained, "He's got lots of guests. Mr. Smith says he'll come with us. He's got a car, and he'll bring Lucy back by nine. OK, Mrs. Ferguson? Oh, what fantastic cakes! Are you having a party, Mrs. Ferguson?"

"Not really," smiled Granny, "but perhaps we'll have one now. Sit down, Lucy and Don, and have some cake and lemonade. I want a word with Grandpa."

She was away some little time, and I discovered later that she had sent Grandpa hurrying off to the phone box to demand a testimonial for Mr. Smith. As he seemed satisfactory in every respect, she returned at last and gave permission for me to go. I was wildly excited, already standing with one foot on the pedal of my bike, but whether at the prospect of seeing a badger, or of meeting a real live author, I was not quite sure.

Then we were off, speeding under the sweeping boughs of the larch trees, which leaned from high up the bank, and I remember thinking there was no joy in the world like the joy of going downhill on a bicycle, with the wind singing in my ears and my hair blown backwards. At the bottom of the hill the meadows broadened out, and we skimmed into the town and pushed our bikes across the cobbles of the old marketplace between the overhanging timbered houses. Don's hotel lay at the far end, and we went round the back to his parents' flat.

"Here's Lucy, Mum," said Don abruptly, disappearing into the next room and leaving me smiling shyly at a stout, comfortable-looking woman. She greeted me with Don's engaging smile and told me to sit down while she finished getting high tea. We were having it early on account of the badgers, whose habits had to be timed very carefully. I sat on the sofa while Don rushed around making preparations for the expedition. You would have thought we were going to the North Pole, from the fuss he made.

And suddenly the door opened, and a voice said quietly, "So you are Lucy, who writes poetry. Good evening, Lucy. I'm Mr. Smith."

I leaped to my feet and then tried hard not to show my disappointment. I had no clear idea of what I had expected an author to look like, but certainly not like the man in the doorway—tall and thin with bowed shoulders, bald on the top of his head, and with a general look of weariness and ill health. But I recovered myself quickly, for his face was very kind, and he looked at me with real interest. I smiled and shook hands and told him I was Lucy, and that I did write stories and poems and things, but they weren't very good.

"They'll improve if you just keep writing," said Mr. Smith, "You must bring them here one day and let me see them. I believe it's teatime now. I'm invited, too, as it's a sort of badger celebration party. Let's go in together."

It really was a party, with ham and salad, fruit and ice cream and cake. Don's dad made all sorts of jokes, and we laughed so much that it was nearing sunset when Mr. Smith, Don, and I finally set off in a great hurry, armed with a flashlight, binoculars, peppermints, and a rug for Mr. Smith, whose health was delicate.

It was about twenty minutes' drive through budding country lanes, but I hardly noticed where we were going because Mr. Smith started talking to me about the books and poems I'd read, almost as though I were an equal. He knew all about *David Copperfield* and *The Wind in the Willows,* and *The Forsaken Merman.* And I found myself talking, too, as I had never talked to any other grown-up before, until I remembered poor Don in the back, who was jigging up and down and dying to give us a lecture on badgers.

"They have their babies down in the setts about February," he began, when he could get a word in edgeways. "Here, this is where we stop, Mr. Smith, up this little lane. You can leave the car in front of the farm, and we go across that field and through that wood, and we'll have to hide in the nettle patch. The sett is just under those bushes. You'll need that rug, Mr. Smith, because of your cough."

He was hurrying across the field, where the daisies

were already closing their petals. The sky above the
hawthorns was faint gold. As we approached the nettle
patch, he went down on all fours and motioned us to
follow and keep perfectly quiet.

I had a feeling that Mr. Smith was not really used to
creeping through brambles and nettles on all fours
like a red Indian stalking his quarry, but he did as he
was told, and we found ourselves in a rather uncom-
fortable little hollow, where we crouched and tried
not to scratch our stings. It was rather cold, and the
dew was falling. I'm sure Mr. Smith was longing to
light a cigarette, but Don had already explained that
this was absolutely forbidden, as the badgers would
almost certainly catch the scent and decide to spend
the evening at home.

The brightness behind the trees faded, and the last
lone thrush stopped singing. We lay so still that we
could hear all sorts of unfamiliar little sounds: the
flight of wings as a bird flew home, the thud of a rab-
bit's back legs in the field behind us. It was getting
dark, and suddenly I felt glad of Mr. Smith's presence
in the ditch beside me and drew a little closer to him.
Don was leaning forward, breathless and absorbed.

And then it happened. A rustle in the dead leaves,
a black nose with a gleaming white stripe—and a large
badger rose up in the dusk, sniffing the air. It lolloped
a few paces, and another appeared. Then they turned
face to face and rose on their hind legs in a kind of
grave twilight dance. Then another and another; an

old fat badger; two small, round, frolicsome badgers tumbling clumsily about, scrambling up molehills and rolling off again. We watched like statues; watched till the lights had gone, and there was nothing more to be seen or heard but ghostly shapes and queer little coughs and snufflings and the rustling of dead leaves—and ourselves, part of their company.

Then Mr. Smith sneezed; and in one second we were alone with the chilly night, the damp ditch, and the stinging nettles.

"I'm most awfully sorry!" said Mr. Smith.

"Don't worry!" said Don generously, suddenly released from his spell. "It was too dark to see them anymore in any case. Wow! Am I stiff! Weren't they fantastic, Mr. Smith? Aren't you glad you came, Lucy? Bet you never saw anything as good as that before! Here, have a peppermint everybody, to warm you up! Don't step in that cowpat, Mr. Smith. Race me to the gate, Lucy!"

He was in tremendous spirits and chattered the whole way home, but I only half listened, because to me the evening had been an almost mystical experience. I knew that I should never forget it as long as I lived—that first upthrust of the striped snout, first one, then another. We had reached my gate, and the moon was flooding the garden, making Grandpa's prize tulips look like pale lanterns.

"Good night, Lucy," said Mr. Smith. "And tomorrow, write about tonight. Write about the birds flying home and the smell of the wet grass; write what you felt when the first badger appeared; write about the moonlight on the tulips. Write it all, and let me see it."

"All right," I said, jumping out of the car, "I'll try. Good night, and thank you very much!" And they left me standing by the gate, wondering how he knew.

CHAPTER SEVEN

A Daring Plan

THE DAYS SPED BY, and the beginning of term put an end to Don's company. We said good-bye in the bluebell wood on a bright spring evening when the westering light, filtering through the young beeches, dappled the pools of blue flowers. Don was perched on a fallen tree trunk, swinging his legs, when he made a disastrous suggestion.

We had been talking about my father again, for the situation had fired Don's imagination. He kept thinking what he would do if *his* dad were in prison.

"If I were you, Lucy," he remarked, "I'd run away and find him. Why don't you, Lucy? You know where the prison is. It's not very far; in fact, I think it's on

59

the main line to London. You could probably get there and back in a day if you looked sharp, and they couldn't stop you. All prisoners are allowed visitors. I asked my dad."

"I couldn't," I said rather crossly. "Granny would never let me. You know she wouldn't."

"You wouldn't tell her, silly," said Don. "You'd have to be going somewhere else and then not go, and then go and see your father instead. You'd probably have to make up some sort of a story, but after all, he's your father, isn't he? If it were mine, nothing would stop me!"

"But I never do go anywhere else," I objected. "And anyhow, I wouldn't have enough money, and anyhow, it's wrong to tell lies, and how would I know the way?"

Don shrugged. "It could probably be worked out," he said. "Think about it, and I'll come and see you when I come home for the weekend in three weeks' time. Cheerio, Lucy! Have a good term!" He gave me a warm, hopeful smile and darted off through the arches of the wood, leaving me trying to forget this most disturbing conversation. But the seed of an idea had been sown, and neither fear, reason, nor conscience could stop its growing.

At first it was easy to forget, because going back to school was always exciting and eventful. During the first week of this term, the result of the prize essay was announced at assembly. To my amazement, I, who had never been anywhere for my summer holidays, had won the prize. I had to walk up and receive it, a book token, and later on Miss Bird read my essay aloud to the English class. I was thrilled, and so were my grandparents. I could hardly wait for Saturday, to show Mr. Smith.

I had started visiting Mr. Smith at the weekend to show him anything I had written, and he, in turn, gave me fresh books or poems to read. He often criticized and seldom praised, but this time he seemed pleased. He read my essay twice through and smiled.

"That's the way, Lucy," he said. "You really experienced this, didn't you? Write the things that you have seen and heard. I believe that comes in the Bible, but I can't tell you where! What are you going to buy with your book token?"

"I don't know," I replied. "Granny said to ask you. Have you any ideas?"

"What about a good young people's anthology?" said Mr. Smith, after thinking for a moment. "I should like to introduce you to some of the more modern poets. One of these days soon I shall be going into town, to buy some books myself. Do you think your grandparents would let you come with me?"

"I'm sure they would," I said enthusiastically. "I'll ask them. Thank you very much, Mr. Smith. I'd love to come."

But that seed of an idea was growing and beginning to fill my mind. In the daytime I was absorbed with my lessons and interests, but the moment Granny had switched off the light and opened the window, my thoughts turned back to Don's suggestion. Some nights I lay awake until nearly midnight, tossing, turning, and planning, for now something had happened that had brought the whole plan actually within the range of possibility.

There was going to be a Whitsun camp leaving early on Whit Saturday morning. We were going to Clee Hill, in Shropshire, and we would pitch our tents, go for a hike, sleep there, parade to church, and come back on Sunday afternoon. The fee for the expedition no doubt would be entrusted to me to deliver, but it would not be enough for my train fare. I had very little pocket money, and my post office savings book was located away in Granny's cash box. Also, where could I stay the night? These two objections seemed quite insuperable, so I gave a sigh of relief, and tried to forget about it once more. With a lightened heart I put down my name for Guide camp and asked if I could share a tent with Mary Blossom again.

But after three weeks Don came home with easy solutions to all my insoluble problems. Money could be got somehow. He would give me some himself, from his bicycle savings. In fact, he produced it from his pocket then and there, and handed it over with a flourish. What was more, if I asked nicely, he was sure Mr. Smith would buy my book token. With my own money, that ought to do me, and the night was no problem, either. He would be home for Whitsun; all

I had to do was take the train to Eastbury, go to the little wood near the hotel, and wait. He would come out every half hour and hoot like an owl, and he would put a blanket and pillow for me in the farm barn behind the house. No one ever went there in the evening and there was plenty of straw for the horse. I could spend a delightful night there with the horse, and wander about the hills next day until it was time to go home. He would smuggle out some food for me, and all would be well.

He was swinging on the gate as he talked. The wind blew his thick hair back from his forehead. His eyes were alight with excitement, and nothing seemed impossible. And yet— I shivered with fright and misery! The wood would be dark and lonely, and I had never slept with a horse before. Besides, what would I say when I got home and my grandparents asked me if I had enjoyed camp?

Even Don owned that this last one was the real snag!

"I think, Lucy, you'll have to tell them," he said seriously. "After all, there's nothing all that wicked in going to see your own dad, but it's better not to tell too many lies. If you told the truth *then*, the lies you had told *before* wouldn't matter any more, would they? And in any case, that army person—"

"Captain," I corrected.

"That Captain person might meet your gran and tell her you hadn't been to camp, and then you'd have had it, wouldn't you!"

"I *couldn't* tell them," I cried.

"Well," said Don patiently, "It's up to you, Lucy. I can't do any more for you. It won't be easy, admitted, but if it was my dad, I'd have a try!"

There were two weeks to go, and the memory of it is rather confused. I only remember lying in bed and hearing the clock strike over and over again, waking heavy-eyed in the morning, and trying to eat when I had no appetite. Whitsun was creeping nearer and nearer, and I could not make up my mind.

I had the money, or would have when Granny gave me my fee for camp. Don had been most efficient in finding out when the train left and the price of a day return. On the Saturday before Whitsun I had taken my book token to Mr. Smith and asked him to buy it, as he needed a book himself. He had looked at me in astonishment, and I could see that he was disappointed.

"But why, Lucy?" he asked. "I thought you were going to buy that anthology. You shouldn't sell your prize."

"I know." I felt my cheeks grow crimson. "But you see, I need the money very badly for something. Please, Mr. Smith, I really do!"

"Can't you tell me what for?"

I shook my head miserably.

"Do your grandparents know?"

"Not yet. I expect they will later."

"Is it for yourself, or for someone else?"

"For someone else."

"Is it for a present?"

"Sort of—not exactly."

"Lucy, couldn't you possibly tell me?"

"Not yet. I will later. I'll come and tell you on Whit Monday, Mr. Smith, honest I will! And it's nothing really naughty."

"Does Don know?"

"Yes, and he doesn't think it's naughty either. He thinks it's something I ought to do."

"I see!" Mr. Smith seemed to have quite a respect for Don's opinions. "Well Don seems a good lad, and I think you're a good girl, too, so I'll trust you. And remember, on Whit Monday you're going to tell me all about it. Here's your money, but I shall keep your book token here in my drawer. You mustn't sell that; it was given you to buy books, not to sell."

Exhausted with relief, I leaned back in the arm-chair and clutched the coins in my pocket. Mr. Smith began talking about ancient Greece, and started to read me Tennyson's *Oenone*. But about ten minutes later, he closed the book.

"You're not paying attention, Lucy," he said gently. "You're far away. I wonder what this big secret is!"

I couldn't concentrate at school, either, and lost marks in all directions. Miss Bird, meeting Granny in town on Thursday, actually asked her if she thought I was quite well. They decided between them that I was worrying about my exams, that the Guide camp would probably do me good, and that I had better have some vitamins.

But I knew that nothing could do me good, and the time was running out fast. I came home from school on Friday evening to find all I needed for camp laid out neatly beside my little rucksack: clothes, bathing things, camp money, and a big bag of sweets. The sweets I would give to my father, but what on earth was I to do with all the other things? I supposed I should have to carry them round on my back until I came home again. Things were getting worse and worse.

I lay awake for a long time, trying to decide what I should say on my return. I knew that Granny's pet abomination in life was "a sly child," and no full-grown fox could be slyer than I was being just then. Only one thought kept me from giving the whole project up: by the time I came home, I would have seen my father, and beyond that, fate would, no doubt, take over.

I slept fitfully, my sleep broken by queer dreams. I had reached the prison, and my father turned away from me. I was back, coming in at the gate, but my grandfather would not look up from his French beans. I awoke, drenched with perspiration. The birds were singing and the sun rising. No retreat now! The sooner I left, the better.

Clad in my Guide uniform, with my rucksack on my back, I swallowed a hasty breakfast and explained that

I had arranged to go to Mary Blossom's house early so that we could start together. Having started on my miserable recital of lies, I felt I wanted to be sick. For one safe moment, I clung to Granny. Her clothes smelt of lavender and mothballs, and the clasp of her arms was infinitely comforting. Then I remembered that I was a sly child, and she might never feel quite the same about me again on my return—unless she need never know. I turned away and ran down the road without a backward look. My great adventure had begun.

Then I heard my name called urgently and turned to see Grandpa, puffing terribly, trotting after me as fast as he could go. What could he want? I was shaking all over when he came up to me, but it was only to slip some money into my hand unseen by Granny, who would have accused him of spoiling me. "For ice cream, Lucy," he panted, "or pop—or whatever you like. Have a good time, dearie."

It was the last straw. I snatched the money and turned away, the tears streaming down my face. But no retreat! There was just one more thing to be done, and then the big risks were behind me. I had written a note to Mary the night before, asking her to tell Captain that I was unexpectedly prevented from coming; I had to go somewhere else. It was a queer, vague little note, but by the time Captain received the message I should be far away.

I crept up to Mary's front door, slipped my note

through the letter box, and darted back to the gate, but there was no escaping Mary. She saw me from the window and came bounding to the front door.

"Lucy, Lucy, wait for me," she yelled. "Why are you running on? We were going together!"

"I can't come" I shouted desperately. "I've got to go somewhere else. Read the note, and tell Captain."

"Can't come?" squealed Mary, "Why not, Lucy? You said you'd come! And if you're going somewhere else, why have you got your Guide uniform on? Lucy, Lucy—wait."

But I had no answer ready and fled down the road, with Mary, too stout to follow at my speed, lamenting at the gate. *That's done it!* I thought to myself. *She'll tell Captain all about me, and they'll know there's something fishy. Perhaps she'll even get in touch with Granny.*

But the bus was coming, and I jumped on and reached the station without incident. I went to the ticket office and asked for a day return to Greening, but having never done such a thing before, I could only speak in a whisper.

"Lost yer voice, luv?" said the man, leaning forward, and I repeated my request in a strange croak that seemed to belong to someone else.

"Over the bridge on number three," said the man. "Now don't lose yer ticket, and enjoy yer 'oliday!"

Down on the platform there was nearly forty minutes to wait, and I ducked behind a large litter bin in case any of my teachers were going away for the weekend. But the coast seemed clear, and at last I actually found myself settled in a corner seat of a third-class compartment, with the train starting up. And then, for better or worse, we were off. I knew it took two and a half hours to get to Greening, but, having no watch, I had no way of marking time, and I amused or annoyed my fellow passengers considerably by seizing my rucksack each time the train drew to a halt and asking, "Excuse me, but is this Greening?"

"Relax, ducks," said a kindly lady when this had happened four times. "I'll tell you in plenty of time to get off at Greening." And after that, I think I must have dropped off to sleep, because the next thing I knew was that she was shaking me gently and we were drawing in to what seemed to be an enormous station. She helped me on with the rucksack and opened the door for me. I stepped out and joined the crowd hurrying to the exit.

CHAPTER EIGHT

At the Prison

ONLY WHEN I GOT OUTSIDE the station and stood in the
busy town street did I realize that I had no idea where
to go. I dreaded asking anyone the way to the prison.
They might guess my secret or even think I had done
something wrong. This worried me so much that I
wasted half an hour plucking up my courage, until,
in the end, I timidly asked a lady who had no idea
where the prison was. Then I asked a boy, not much
older than myself, who looked friendly, but he
laughed, and asked me what I'd been an' gone an'
done, and how many years I'd got, and went off whistling.

It was well past one o'clock by now, and I was get-ing desperate. I was being jostled in the street, and yet I had never before felt so completely alone. I looked round and saw an old lady selling flowers. Gathering up my courage, I crossed to her.

"Can you tell me the way to the prison?" I whispered shamefacedly.

"Prison, love?" she queried. "That's not far from here. Go up to the end of that street over there, and take bus number eight. It'll take you right close. Then ask again."

I ran all the way and jumped on number eight, which was just passing. It was crowded, and I had to wait for my ticket.

"Prison, dear?" said the conductor. "You're going the wrong way, and this is a one-way street. You'll have to get off at the next stop, cut up Church Street, and catch the number eight going back. They go right past the prison."

I could almost write a book about my misfortunes in Greening alone. I cut down Church Street instead of up it, and got lost for quite a time before I found the right bus stop, where I was told the number eight had just gone. Standing waiting in the road, I realized I had had no dinner and very little breakfast and was desperately hungry. I trotted off to a shop and bought myself a bun, some chocolate, and pop, but I took longer than I meant to choosing what I wanted, and when I got back I saw the next bus disappearing around the corner.

I knew by this time that I was unlikely to catch the train that Don had told me to catch, but this did not particularly worry me. For by the time I needed to decide anything, I would have seen my father. When the next bus rolled up, I felt fortified by the picnic and strangely at peace. Only a little longer, and I would hand over the responsibility of this wild expedition into my father's hands. He would tell me what to do.

"Prison up top of the street next to the church," shouted the conductor, and I was glad to dismount, for I felt all eyes upon me. But as I hurried toward it, my heart was as light as air. I had done it; I had arrived! I thought of Don. "I don't care what you did, Dad," I whispered to myself. "I'm your girl, and I've come."

The entrance was quite obvious, an enormous door in a high stone wall that enclosed a yard with buildings within, and a smaller door with a grid set in it. The bell was out of reach—I was rather small for my age—so I knocked hard with my fists. No one answered at first, so I went on knocking, and my heart began to beat rather fast. Supposing visiting hours were over? I started kicking rather wildly, and at last the grid above my head opened and a voice said, "Hullo?"

"Hullo," I answered, standing away from the door so as to be seen. "I've come to visit my father, Mr. Martin. He's been here about nine years, and I'm Lucy Martin, his daughter."

"Sorry," said a voice, "It's not visiting day today,

and children aren't let in alone. Ask your Mum to
bring you next time."

I could hardly believe my ears! I simply stared as
the grid closed, and then I panicked. I ran at the door,
kicking, hammering with my fists and shouting at the
top of my voice. "Don't go away! Please, please, don't
go away; I haven't got a mother, and I've come alone.
Oh, please let me in! He's my father!"

I didn't notice the passersby forming into a little
crowd to stare at me, but one lady, who thought, no
doubt, that my father had just been locked up, tried
to persuade me to come away. I pushed her aside and
continued my mad assault, and in the end she rang the
bell above my head and the grid opened again.

"Can someone speak to this little girl?" said the
lady. "She seems very much upset and quite alone."

I heard footsteps receding across the courtyard, and
the lady put her arm round my shivering little figure,
trying to quiet me. Then we heard the sound of footsteps approaching, a key turned in a lock, and the
little door set in the big door opened. A large man in
a navy blue uniform stood looking down at me. "Now,
now!" he said, "What's all this to-do?"

"It's my father," I gulped. "He's here. I came all
the way from Eastbury to see him, and you won't let
me in. And I don't know where to go now, and I think
I've missed the last train home. And oh, please! I
came all by myself—and I *must* see him. Please, please,
please let me in!"

The officer looked down at me thoughtfully, and I'm sure I looked a most pitiful sight. "You'd best step inside," he said kindly. "We'll see what can be done."

I pressed through the open door without a backward look, and he led me into a small office just inside and pointed me to a chair.

"Now," he said. "Tell me all about it. What's your name, and who's your dad?"

I told him everything. I poured out my story, confident that if only he knew all, he could not refuse me. He was a patient man. He listened right through to the end without interrupting once. "And I know he's a bad man," I finished with a gulp, "or he wouldn't be here at all, but after all, he is my father—and I—I—well, we haven't seen each other for eight years and he wants me. He said so."

The warden rose and sat down at the desk. He pulled out an enormous ledger.

"John Martin," he murmured, turning the pages. Then he sat for a time gazing thoughtfully down at the book, as though uncertain as to what to say next.

"Your dad wasn't a bad man," he said at last. "We were all very fond of your dad. Reg'lar nice chap he was. But the trouble is—he's not here. He behaved so well, he got let out early. Left here beginning of April!"

For a moment I sat rigid with shock, as the real meaning of this dawned on me. All the needless de-

ception and fear, all the wasted money, and all the
dilemma of what to do next meant nothing to me.
Only one thing mattered. My father had been out of
prison for over two months, and he had never been
near me or asked for me. It was all a terrible mistake.
He didn't want me at all. I had no father. I crumpled
up in the armchair and cried as though my heart
would break.

The kind warden was quite upset but had no idea
what to do. He lumbered off, scratching his head, and
returned with some tea and cake and a picture paper
and told me to cheer up, as he was fetching a lady who
would put things right in no time. I tried to sip the
tea, but my tears still flowed freely, and I cried until I
could cry no more. When a lady in a blue uniform arrived (I discovered later that she was a social worker
and her name was Miss Dixon) I was lying back perfectly quiet and half asleep. I had given up on what
was to happen next.

The lady seemed more sure of herself than the
warden, and acted as though dealing with broken-
hearted children was all part of her day's work. She
asked me a few questions and then remarked that what
I needed was a meal and a good sleep, and she was
going to take me home for the night. Her cheerful
common sense reassured me, and I pulled myself together and followed her out to the car. In any case, it
was a relief to be taken somewhere, as I had vaguely

pictured myself pacing the streets until morning or perhaps sleeping in the waiting room at the station.

"I'm going to phone your grandparents, Lucy," she said as we drove through the streets. "I'm sure they'd like to come and fetch you tomorrow morning."

But I worked myself into quite a state when she said that and assured her that we didn't have a phone and that I had my return ticket and could easily get home alone. The appearance of an angry granny in Greening, all mixed up with Miss Dixon and the warden, seemed too complicated to be even considered. She seemed to accept this, and we soon arrived at her flat.

I know it was cheerful and comfortable, and I'm sure Miss Dixon gave me a good meal, but I was too tired and confused and unhappy to register much. I know that by the end of supper I could hardly keep my eyes open, and I believe she found my pajamas in my rucksack and helped me into bed.

Only just as I was dropping off, she put her hand on my shoulder and said: "Lucy, it won't be at all hard to find your father. There are records kept of all prisoners, and we should be able to trace him at once. But you must tell me your address, so he'll know where to find you."

I fell into the trap at once. "Pheasant Cottage, Eastwood Estate, Eastbury," I murmured drowsily, and I remember thinking that there was no point in tracing my father. If he had loved me, he would have come alone. I didn't want to see him any more. I did not have a father. I fell asleep.

When I woke late next morning I could not imagine where I was. Instead of bird song and the rustling of summer trees, I could hear buses and cars, and a girl stood at the bottom of my bed whom I never remembered seeing before. She wore a summer dress, and her hair fell loose over her shoulders. It was only when I was halfway through my breakfast that I realized she was the same person as Miss Dixon in uniform the night before.

She told me she had looked up the Sunday trains, and the next one left at twelve. Then she cleared her throat and said carefully, "Lucy, I felt last night that I needed to have a talk with your grandparents, so I phoned up—"

I stiffened in my seat. "You couldn't!" I protested. "They don't have a phone."

"No, but I sent a police message asking them to phone me," replied Miss Dixon quietly, "and we had a long talk. They will meet you at the station, but there's nothing to be worried about. They understand now about your wanting to see your father—"

"I don't want to see my father," I muttered, "and I'm not worried." Then because tears were near, I gulped down my tea and went to pack my rucksack, and she, sensibly, left me alone. I sat looking in silence at a book until it was time to go to the station, and only when the train came roaring in did I realize how very, very kind Miss Dixon had been. I tried to stammer out my thanks and tell her I was sorry. But she smiled and seemed to understand that I had not been quite myself. So I waved to her out of the window and then settled down in my corner for the journey.

But the green Cotswold countryside and the crimson flashes of rambling roses against old gray stone gave me no pleasure. My brave expedition had failed utterly, and I was just a sly, weary child going home to hear what Granny thought of me. I sat staring dully out of the window until the train stopped at Eastbury, and there were Granny and Grandpa hurrying forward to meet me. Even I noticed how white and old they looked, and how dark were the circles under Granny's eyes.

I braced myself for the storm, but there was nothing to be afraid of. Miss Dixon's talk had had a queer effect on them, for they seemed to be treating me like a visitor, making conversation about small matters that had nothing to do with the wickedness and deceit of the past twenty-four hours. Grandpa looked acutely miserable and kept blowing his nose, but he spoke cheerfully, and Granny had made a special cake for tea. It was all most strange, and I even found myself longing to be scolded.

Don arrived after tea. He seemed rather shy at meeting Granny, so he rang his bicycle bell at the gate until I saw him and rushed out with Shadow barking a welcome at my heels. Don's eyes were nearly popping out of his head with excited curiosity.

"Whatever happened?" he began. "Didn't you go? I got the bedding over to the stable right under my mum's nose, and she never noticed, and I went to the wood and hooted about a hundred times."

"Yes, I did go," I replied. "Come up the hill, and I'll tell you all about it."

He parked the bike inside the gate, and we climbed the hillside to a favorite place of mine, an outcrop of rock around which thyme and sorrel and bedstraw grew like a garden. There we settled down, and I told him every detail of my great adventure.

"Bet your gran was mad with you!" said Don, thoughtfully chewing a bracken stem.

"No, she wasn't," I replied slowly, fondling Shadow's ears. She didn't say anything. I think Miss Dixon told her not to. But it was all for nothing, Don. He's been out over two months, and he hasn't come. I suppose he just didn't want to be bothered with me, after all."

Don shook his head slowly.

"He'll come," he said. "Perhaps he's ill, or perhaps he wants to earn some money or find a home first or something. Fathers always want their children. Which reminds me, Dad's going to help me with my Latin tonight, so I'd better go."

We raced down the hill and he pedaled away, whistling. *Happy Don,* I thought to myself, *speeding toward his beloved dad!* I sighed and went into the house, thankful that it was nearly bedtime.

Granny came up as usual, but there was still no mention of her opinions of sly children. She kissed me good night and then lingered as though she wanted to say something but could not find the right words. An unusual difficulty for Granny!

"Lucy," she said at last, "I'm sorry you couldn't tell us. But never mind about that now. But I want you to understand that if your father ever turns up, we will never try to stop him from seeing you. You are free to choose. We shall pray God you'll choose rightly.

She turned away and seemed to grope for the door, leaving me speechless and dismayed. What did it all mean? Had I been such a sly child that they did not want me anymore? Had I run after a love that had never existed, only to forfeit the strong love I already possessed? My safe little world seemed to be crumbling all round me, and I panicked. "Granny, Granny," I cried, and jumped out of bed and tiptoed downstairs to find them both. I had no idea what to say. I just had to get to them.

But on the bottom step I stopped as though turned to stone at a sound I had never heard before. Granny was crying, and between her sobs I heard her say in a broken voice, "Oh, Herbert, Herbert, whatever should we do without her?"

I turned and crept back upstairs. I had found my answer. I jumped into bed and fell deeply and peacefully asleep.

CHAPTER NINE

A Strange Journey

WE HAD A HOLIDAY on Whit Monday, and I went to see Mr. Smith. I found him, as usual, bent over his manuscripts and looking tired and worried. But he always seemed glad to see me and always found time to share some new poem or story that he had enjoyed.

"Well, Lucy," he said, "have you come to tell me about your great secret?" He flung himself back in a comfortable chair, and I perched happily on the arm, because I had gradually come to talk to Mr. Smith as I talked to no other grown-up, without any reserve at all.

"Well, yes," I replied, "I'll tell you now because it's

81

all over. But I shall have to begin right at the beginning and tell you about my father. You see he did something very wicked when I was about three and he went to prison."

I glanced at him anxiously to see whether he was very shocked, but he only said, "Go on; tell me more."

So I told him my story all over again, just as I had told Don and the warden, and, like them, he listened quietly until I had nearly finished—so quietly, with his head so bowed, that I thought perhaps he was asleep and stopped talking.

"Have you gone to sleep?" I asked softly.

He looked up quickly. "No, I'm not asleep," he said. "I'm just listening. But Lucy, tell me this. If he was such a bad man, why do you want to see him again? You're happy with your grandparents. Wouldn't it be better to forget all about him?"

My eyes filled with tears. This was what I had sometimes reasoned out myself, but Don and my own heart told me that my reason was wrong. And I had risked so much—and all for nothing. I clenched my fists.

"He's my daddy, isn't he?" I almost shouted. "And even if he has been bad I'm still—" I could get no further, for the tears were streaming down my face. Mr. Smith pulled a handkerchief out of his pocket and handed it to me, and after a few moments I was able to go on.

"I didn't forget him. I went—and it was terribly difficult. But he's forgotten me. He's been out two months now, and he hasn't come. If he'd wanted me, he'd have come quick, wouldn't he?"

Mr. Smith leaned forward and laid his hand on my knee. "He'll come, Lucy," he said quietly. "And he'll be a lucky man to find such a brave, faithful, loyal little daughter waiting for him. You see, when people come out of prison, they are sometimes ashamed and afraid. After all, from what you say, your grandparents don't seem to think much of him, do they? What would they do, if he came?"

"They—they said I could choose," I sniffed. "But they wouldn't want me to go. And—well—he was a bad man, wasn't he, to have gone to prison? And they want me to grow up good. And I couldn't leave them; I wouldn't know what to do!"

Tears were still close, for the whole problem seemed too great to be solved, and I didn't know where to turn. But Mr. Smith could not tell me what to do either. He only said, "He was a bad man eight years ago, Lucy, but eight years is a long time. People sometimes change, especially when they have little girls waiting for them. Don't worry; I think he will come in his own time, and when he comes, you'll know what to do all right."

When I got home, the house was empty because my grandparents had gone to a flower show to exhibit Grandpa's prize sweet peas. Shadow came running out, wagging his tail and barking at my bicycle. He hated my bicycle, because it meant that he could not come with me. I flung myself down on the daisies and hugged him hard, for although he could not tell me what to do, he was very comforting. Granny had often told me to pray when I was in trouble, but I could never feel there was really anyone there listening. Or if there was, He was so far away that my words could not possibly reach Him.

Long ago, when I was a tiny child, I had gone to a house with Granny and she had phoned Grandpa, who was ill in hospital. As soon as she had left the room, I too had lifted the receiver and begun to chatter excitedly to Grandpa, and when Granny had come back she had found me crying because he wouldn't answer. She had lifted me on to her lap and explained about disconnected telephones. Sometimes now, when I said my prayers, I thought of that disconnected telephone.

Perhaps He did not listen because I had been so deceitful. With my cheek pressed against Shadow's back, I made up my mind to try and be very good, to say my prayers every night, to listen in church instead of making up stories, and to read the Bible even though it did not interest me. I decided to help more in the house and garden instead of always running off to play as soon as I decently could, and to work hard at subjects which I did not like. I would never again tell a lie or answer back or pretend I hadn't finished my homework so as to stay up later. Granny had often told me that if I was really good, the help I needed would be given me, so I resolved to try out what she said.

I tried hard to keep these good resolutions. The rest of the term passed peacefully, for my grandparents appreciated my efforts, and my math teacher said she could not imagine what had come over Lucy. But deep within I knew that nothing had really happened. I tried reading my Bible, but it seemed an old, dead book. In fact church, the Bible, and praying seemed like three roads that led into a thick mist that I could not penetrate. Whether there was some goal beyond the mist or whether the roads just petered out, I had no way of telling. Granny and Grandpa were devout churchgoers who practiced their religion but seldom talked about it, and I knew of no words with which to bring up the subject.

And in the meantime the question persisted like a nagging toothache: *If he suddenly comes, what, oh what shall I do?*

I did well in my end-of-term exams, and on the first day of the holidays Mr. Smith fulfilled his promise and took me to town in his car to change my book token for a book. Granny had never met Mr. Smith—he seemed shy of coming to the cottage—but because Don's father spoke so highly of him, she let me visit him when I pleased. She saw me off at the gate after breakfast. I remember turning at the corner of the road and thinking how safe and kind she looked under the arch of crimson ramblers. Neither of us had the slightest idea that this was to be the most eventful day in my whole life and that nothing would ever be quite the same again.

The expedition started brightly. It was a perfect morning. I stuck my head out of the window, and sniffed at the warm scents of summer; the new-mown hay and honeysuckle, the good smells of farms and beanfields. Late wild roses danced in the hedges alongside early foxgloves, and I sang softly to myself because it was the first day of the holidays, the sun was scattering the heat haze, and I was going to town with Mr. Smith.

"Happy, Lucy?" he asked suddenly.

I smiled and nodded. We were reaching the outskirts of the town, where the cathedral towered rocklike above the shining river. We parked in its shadows and spent a long time in Smith's selecting my book— an anthology of poems called *The Dragon Book of Verse*. Then we had ice cream and visited the cathedral, and Mr. Smith told me about Norman and Gothic architecture and pointed out wonders in stone that I would never have noticed by myself. We visited King John's tomb and discussed the Magna Carta, and when we finally came out blinking into the sunshine, it was past dinner time. So we went to the market and had ham sandwiches, custard tarts, and lemonade.

But in spite of all these delights, and in spite of his real love of the cathedral, I could not help noticing how ill Mr. Smith looked. He left his sandwich almost untasted and kept coughing in a nervous, worried way. By the time we reached the car, he seemed to be breathing faster than usual, and as we left the town I thought we were also driving faster than usual.

"We're going home a different way," I observed. "Is it quicker?"

He did not answer; he merely drove faster, and after a time I noticed, to my great surprise, that our hills, which rose like a barrier across the plain, were getting smaller and farther away. Instead of driving toward them, we were driving away from them.

"Mr. Smith," I said, puzzled but still unalarmed, "where are we going? This isn't the way home. The hills are behind us."

But again he did not answer, and I think it was at this point that a cold trickle of fear crept into my mind, and I became vaguely uneasy. Why didn't he answer? Why were we driving so fast? And why did he look so white and strange? Was I being kidnapped? Suddenly the fear broke loose and I seized his arm.

"Mr. Smith," I shouted, "where are we going? I want to go home, and you're going the wrong way."

He slowed up at once and drew the car onto the grass at the side of the road. For a moment we sat in tense silence then he turned to me with that gentle smile I had come to love. I knew that I was perfectly safe with him and wondered how I could ever have been afraid.

"Lucy," he said very quietly, "do you ever still think about that bad father of yours?"

I nodded, staring. Perhaps at that moment I began to understand.

"Lucy, what would you do if he ever turned up?"

I just went on staring. Light was dawning. Old memories were stirring. Not a white weary face but a brown, laughing face looking back over his shoulder. I was riding a horse, and the skies were very blue. The faces were coming into focus, and he was speaking again.

"Lucy, I'm your father. I wanted us to get to know each other before I told you. I've written to your grandparents; Don's father took the letter up at dinner time. I've asked them if they'll spare you for a few weeks. I want you to come away with me, if you will."

I could not speak, because the thing for which I had been waiting, half hoping, half dreading, had happened, and it wasn't the least bit like what I had expected. Only one thing was really clear to me: my father had come after all. He hadn't forsaken me. He had been there all the time. I realized that I had loved and trusted this man from the moment I had set eyes on him, and now I understood why. For a moment my gladness seemed to be lifting me up high into the sparkling air. Then I came down to earth with a bump, for my father was speaking.

"Lucy," he said, "will you come with me?"

"Yes, if Granny will let me."

"But I don't think Granny will let you, or at least she would persuade you not to. I want you to come now. I've told your grandparents in the letter to be at the Roman Camp Hotel at half past three, and I will phone them and talk it over. After all, I'm your father; I have the right—if you'll come."

"But I can't. I must go home. I haven't got my pajamas and toothbrush."

"We'll buy all you need in the next town. Will you come?"

"But I can't. I haven't said good-bye to Granny and Grandpa."

"But if we go back, you won't come at all. You could say good-bye on the phone. Tell them you want to go just for a few weeks. I've promised faithfully to bring you back before school."

"But I can't. They'd be so sad, and Granny would be so cross."

"I'm not sure that they'll be either now that they've read my letter. They knew it was coming, and I think they may be very relieved that I want you to stay with them during term time. They've done very well by you, and that's a good school you go to. You must finish there. I only want you for a holiday at present, and I might have asked for you altogether. But of course, it is really up to you. We can say good-bye on the phone and go straight on, or, if you decide against it, we'll turn back. I can drop you near the gate and go on. My luggage is in the trunk, and I'm leaving today."

"But why won't you come in and talk?"

"Because your Granny said long ago that she never wanted to see me again. And if we talk, you'll give in and stay. You couldn't stand up to them. They've brought you up too well. So it's now or never. Will you come?"

I was silent, and I knew he was watching me as though his life depended on it. This was the moment I had dreaded, and I felt torn in half. Pictures seemed to flash on the screen of my mind—little, forgotten scenes, all crystal clear: Granny waiting at the bus stop as I came out of Primary school; Grandpa leaning over the gate and peering into the dusk for my home-coming; Shadow prancing down the path; and many more, like strong tendrils drawing me back to the old, secure, obedient life. I looked up imploringly and shook my head.

And then a last scene, clearer than all the others. Don, standing among the daffodils with the burgeoning wood behind him, green and gold, his head thrown back, his hazel eyes very bright. Clear as a bugle blast, his voice challenged me, "I should find him some-where, somehow, and I should say to him, 'I don't care what you've done, Dad, I'm still your boy.' "

I drew a deep breath and nodded.

"I'll come," I whispered, "when I've phoned Granny and Grandpa."

His tired face relaxed. "Thank you, Lucy," he said. "There's a hotel in the next town, and we'll phone from there."

We drove on in silence, and I leaned my spinning head against his shoulders and tried to take in that this was my father. We stopped at an inn called The Cat and Compasses, and he ordered tea for me while he went to phone. He was away a long time, but when he came back he looked brighter. "Come quick," he said. "I've left the receiver off for you."

I was not very accustomed to talking on phones, and I hardly knew what to say. "Granny, Grandpa," I cried, "do you mind? Please say I can go! You see, he was my father all the time. Granny, Grandpa it's only for a few weeks. I'm coming back for certain sure, and I'll write to you every day."

"Lucy, Lucy!" It was Granny's voice urgent and pleading. "Do you really want to go? He won't take you against your wishes. Just tell him."

"But Granny, I must go. You see, he's my father, and he's not a bad man. It was all a mistake, and he's a good man now. Granny, Grandpa, I'm sorry, but we must give him a chance, mustn't we? Grandpa—"

"God keep you, our darling child!" it was Grandpa's voice, distressed but firm. "Don't be troubled about us, Lucy. It had to come. Only write often and come back. Now good-bye!"

"Good-bye Granny. Good-bye Grandpa. Write to me. Kiss Shadow, and tell Don." I was frantically kissing the receiver, but my father, who was standing behind me, took it gently from me and laid it down.

"I think that's enough," he said. "They understand, and they are glad that it's only for a holiday. Now we must be on our way."

I jumped into the car and we were off, and my heart was in a turmoil of sorrow, relief, regret, excitement, and a wild sense of freedom. The hills and all they stood for were far behind us now, and there was no turning back. What lay ahead I had not yet thought to ask.

In front of us the road rose to a bright horizon; and beyond that? I suddenly began to wonder and turned toward him.

"Mr. Smith—I mean, Daddy—where are we going?

"To London tonight," he replied. "And tomorrow we must take your photograph and finish off your passport. We are flying to the south of Spain. I've got your ticket in my pocket. You'll be able to swim in the blue Mediterranean, and we'll stay with your old nurse. She's longing to see you."

But once again I was struck speechless and simply stared. The day after tomorrow I was going to see the sea!

CHAPTER TEN

My Father's Story

TWO DAYS LATER, not long before sunset, I stood completely dazed and bewildered in the hot southern airport, marveling at the speed and fluency of the Spanish language that was being gabbled all around me. Out of the window of the plane I had watched the vast expanse of the sea, and as soon as my father had collected the luggage—he and I had done some very necessary shopping in London the day before—we were to travel in the bus along the coast, and I would see it again to my heart's content. And tomorrow I would swim in it! This fact alone filled my thoughts to the exclusion of all else, and my father had to tap me on the shoulder to gain my attention.

"Wake up, Lucy," he said; "The bus is nearly full." We jumped into the two last seats, and the bus rattled off toward the town. I sat silent, trying to take in the great hills storming the hot sunset sky, the silhouettes of palm trees black against the rose, the amazing number of people in the streets and gardens, and, above all, the thin silver horizon eastward, beyond the port, where the sun still touched the sea.

By the time we had transferred our luggage to another bus and started our journey south, it was almost dark, but the darker it grew the livelier the streets became. We kept rattling through colorful little coastal towns, where lights streamed from every shop window, and people ate and drank and danced and played guitars and sold their wares on the pavements. Then, about an hour later, the bus drew up in a cobbled square, and my father said, "Come on, Lucy. Here we are."

We gathered up our luggage and pushed our way through the bright, jostling streets until we came to a long, low house a little way out of town. It was a sort of bar, and once again people sat all over the pavement laughing and eating shrimps and olives, and drinking wine. We went around to a door at the side, and my father knocked.

The next moments were rather confusing. The door was opened instantly, and I saw, against the orange glow of the kitchen, a sea of dark, eager faces and shining dark eyes. A voice cried, "Lucita, Lucita," followed by a torrent of Spanish. A woman had thrown her arms round me, was holding me close, and was kissing me over and over again, and somehow the clasp of her arms and the sound of her voice were not entirely unfamiliar. Long, long ago, under some very blue skies—

We somehow all got into the kitchen, and she was holding me at arm's length, half laughing, half crying, and a pretty, dark-haired girl in a pinafore was stroking my hair and smiling shyly. Three more dark, shiny-eyed little children were pressing into the circle. My father laughed.

"Don't look so surprised, Lucy," he said. "This is your old nurse, Lola, and this is Rosita, who was born the same month as you. You shared her cot! And this is Pepito, who was a fat baby when I last saw him. The others I don't know yet, but you'll soon learn to understand them."

"Pedro, Conchita," said Lola proudly, thrusting them forward, "and Francisco," she added, pulling a sleepy, blinking baby out of a crib in the next room and holding him up. Then she dumped him in Rosita's arms and turned to my father, jabbering, laughing, gesticulating with her hands. To my great surprise, my father appeared to understand and jabbered back.

So we were somehow escorted by the whole family to two whitewashed rooms at the back of the house opening onto a courtyard roofed by a great vine (I discovered later that it was called a patio), with a low table in the middle of it set for supper. Supper also was brought in by the whole family: potato omelettes; bottles of wine; yellow, rather greasy rice with shrimps and other strange morsels in it; and great red slices of watermelon.

But the heat and the smell of oil were making me feel rather giddy, and before my father had finished eating, Lola was helping me to bed. But before I lay down, I opened the window that looked out onto the beach and heard the sound of small waves breaking and drawing back over pebbles. Tomorrow—tomorrow—

The sun streaming into the room and the cries of the fishermen woke me early next morning, and I rushed to the window. I could not stick my head out, because there was an iron grill, but I inhaled the salt, fishy air and leaned my arms on the sill to watch the pulling in of the nets and the excited sorting of the catch. To me it was as fascinating as a play, and I think I would have kneeled there for hours watching the sparkling sea and the busy beach had not Rosita put her head around the door and pointed severely to my clothes.

"*Venga,*" she said, and signaled to me to come.

I lost no time in getting ready. My father, in the room on the other side of the patio, was still asleep. It was quite early, and the bar was being cleaned by a singing girl. I was quite dazzled by the morning light in the streets and the colors of the little town: blue-tiled benches in the square, rows of orange trees, scarlet geraniums in the windows, purple and crimson bouganvilia on white walls.

Rosita and I linked arms and went to the baker's, where we bought enormous loaves. Then we went on to a stall on the pavement where a man was frying batter, squeezing ribbons of paste around and around in the hot fat until it was nearly the size of a cartwheel, and Rosita bought the family breakfast. And wherever we went, she introduced me proudly with a little bow and flourish as *"Lucita—mi amiga."*

It was the first of many happy mornings, for life in Spain followed a happy pattern. Early each morning I shopped with Rosita and then had breakfast with my father. After breakfast we sat at the table under the vine and read poetry or history or other literature, and sometimes he gave me an essay to write. Then I left him to his own writing and went over to the inn to help Rosita with her many household chores or took Francisco for a walk or played with Conchita on the beach.

I had never met such a busy child as Rosita, and Lola, who looked after the family and mostly ran the inn, was glad for my help. When I asked Rosita by signs and a few acquired words why her father could not run the inn, she tipped an imaginary bottle to her lips and indicated that he was usually in no condition to do anything at all.

I dined with my father. He often looked weary and ill after a morning's writing and seemed out of breath, but he was always gentle and glad for my company. Over our meal and after dinner, when it was too hot to go out, we held long conversations on many different subjects. Only one subject we had never touched on, and I used to think it lay between us until one afternoon, when I was lying on a mattress in the shade of the vine and he was leaning back smoking, we suddenly found ourselves talking about it.

"Daddy," I said, "did Mummy know Lola and Rosita?"

He nodded. "They were great friends, and both expecting their first babies at the same time. I was brought up in Spain. My father was in the consulate, and I thought there was nowhere like it. I wanted your mother to love it too, and we kept a most successful little guesthouse just across the way. When you were born and she died, Lola fed you and brought you up with Rosita. I gave up the business, came here to this room as a paying guest, and tried to get on with my writing. But I think I had ceased to care about anything, except you, and I didn't write much."

"But why didn't you go to Granny and Grandpa?"

"Your grandparents are excellent people, Lucy, but they had no use for me. They wanted a square man with a steady job for their daughter, and when she married me secretly, against their wishes, they more or less cut me off. I'm not so sure about the old man, but she wears the trousers, doesn't she? Alice planned to take you home on a visit; she was sure it would all blow over then—she could never endure to be on bad terms with anybody. Sure enough, when she died they tried hard to get in touch. But at that point I suppose you might say I cut them off. I only knew one thing clearly then, and that was that I wanted to keep you by me. You're very like her, Lucy, and I always wished I'd known her as a child and could have watched her grow up."

"And then?"

"How much have your grandparents told you?"

"Only what I told you. I asked Grandpa, but he didn't know much—just something about drugs—and that you went to prison."

"Right! I'll tell you everything. I met the agent by chance in a café, although I think now that he'd been shadowing me for a long time. I was just the man he wanted. I'd lived in Spain for years, knew the language, needed money badly, and was half crazy with grief. At first it all seemed quite small, and by the time I realized what a big affair it was, it was too late to pull out. They have their own ways of dealing with defectors. Besides, in a way, I was quite enjoying it!"

"But why did you enjoy it when it was so wicked?"

He looked rather sad. "I didn't think about the wickedness then. I was so desperate without your mother I just wanted something to make me forget; I didn't care very much what. Smuggling was dan-

gerous and exciting, and I didn't stop to think about
what I was handling. It brought me lots of money, too.
I bought a car for myself and teddy bears for you and
Rosita." He laughed and lit another cigarette.

"And then?"

"Well, it all got bigger and bigger, until I realized
I was involved in a huge international heroin ring.
By then, as I said, it was too late to get out. I did it for
three years, taking bigger and bigger risks. My big
mistake was going to England to meet an agent. The
police were waiting for me at the airport, and that was
that. I'm glad I wasn't taken in Spain, or I might
never have been allowed back."

"And then you went to prison?"

"Well, they let me settle you up with your grandparents first, and then, yes, I was sent to prison for ten
years, but they cut it down to eight."

"Well," I said thoughtfully, "I don't think it was all
that wicked. I mean, it's not as bad as stealing or killing people, is it?"

My father became serious. "Lucy," he said, "to start
someone on drugs is far, far worse than killing him
outright. I soon realized that when I got to prison and
had time to think. Never, never have anything to do
with it."

"Then were you very sorry in prison? Wasn't it very
nasty?"

"Well, I don't know. You mustn't think prisons in
England are cruel places. I spent a lot of time in the

infirmary, where I was very well treated indeed. But the evenings were pretty bad, locked in those cells with nothing to do but think. Fortunately, I had my writing. I had plenty to write about by that time, and that kind of adventure story sells well. What really made me sorry was missing you growing up, and all through my own stupid fault."

"But weren't you ever sorry because—well, sort of—because of God?"

"God, Lucy? Believe in God if you like, but He never did much for me except take my wife. No, I was sorry about the lives I'd helped to ruin, and I wanted to be different because of you. You're all I've got now. Old friends kind of disappear when you come out of prison. There's only you."

"But why didn't anyone tell me? Then I could have come and seen you."

"I agreed with your grandparents that it was far better for you not to know while you were little. It's no fun having a father in prison whom you're ashamed of. Children ask questions. You'd never have felt safe."

"But why didn't you tell us it was you when you came out?"

"Because I wanted to introduce myself and get to know you in my own way. If your grandparents had known, they'd have turned you right against me, wouldn't they? You know they would."

His voice was hard and bitter, and I was vaguely

uneasy, because Granny would have considered this shocking talk. But somehow talking to Daddy was quite different from talking to Granny, or even Grandpa. Granny knew all the answers and always told me what I ought to think about everything; and if I happened to think differently, then I was wrong, and it had always seemed very peaceful and safe.

But this man with his sad, questioning eyes and wounded past did not know all the answers, and he wanted me to think and find out for myself. That remark about God, for instance; I felt all the old foundations of my life trembling. I must think and find out for sure.

Our talk was interrupted by an excited knocking on the door, and Pepito burst in with a letter.

"Lucita!" he shouted and thrust it at me. It was my second letter from my grandparents, and a mild rush of homesickness came over me as I took it, as though they were stretching out steadying hands across the miles. I stood up. "I'm going under the trees opposite to read my letter," I said, and Daddy smiled and nodded. I left him persuading Pepito that he need not follow me and that I would share the news on my return.

I knew where to go. If you turned inland and followed a high, white wall, you came to a narrow thicket of eucalyptus trees. Beyond were a few tumbledown little houses on the edge of the vineyards and a dirt track leading to a farm, an old stone cross, and a plantation of olive trees. This was the shadiest place I knew, and I headed toward it clutching my precious letter.

People who lived near the inn were beginning to know me, and I had already picked up a few words of Spanish and enjoyed greeting people in the friendly Spanish way. But today the neighborhood was very quiet, for the grape harvest had not yet begun, and the children were working in the fields or playing on the beach. Only one old woman dressed in black sat at the door of her house with a tortoiseshell cat beside her. She was cleaning a tray with sand and watching a goat.

I bade her good afternoon and then hesitated. Something about her reminded me of Granny. For the first time since arriving in Spain, I felt very homesick, and the shadow of the future loomed larger, for soon I would have to take sides.

I turned back to the old woman and found her looking at me, her brown, wrinkled face beaming with love. I was strangely attracted, and when she moved up, I sat down on the step beside her and stroked the cat. This pleased her, and she turned and opened the door of the cabin and pointed to a basket of kittens under the table.

I went in to play with them for a few minutes, and as I did so I looked around. The room was very bare and very clean; just a quilted bed, a rush mat, a table and chair, a box, and on it a black book that looked like Granny's family Bible. I looked at it more closely. It *was* a Bible—the words *La Biblia* were engraved in gold on the cover. So this old woman believed in God, and if what Granny said was true, God was the only person who could help me. I must keep on thinking and finding out, and perhaps when I knew more Spanish I could come and talk to this woman.

So I said good-bye, and she stroked my hair and made signs to me to come again. I nodded, and trotted off along the dirt track, where blue stars of chicory, climbing convolvulus, and great purple thistles still bloomed in the scorched grass. The farm was surrounded by high walls and smelled of pigs and goats and wild thyme and peppermint. A friendly, white pig wandered out and began rooting in the dust. I sat down under an olive tree and began to read.

They had both written. Granny's part was full of good advice, imploring me to wash my hair regularly, to be careful in the sea, never to go out alone, and to come back as soon as possible. "We pray for you daily," it ended, "and commit you to God's care. I don't suppose there'll be an English church, but say your prayers every night, and trust in your heavenly Father." Grandpa's letter was full of anxious love interspersed with news about the marrows and Shadow, the cat and the church festival, all the little bits of home chat I wanted to hear. I sat for a long time devouring my letters, chewing over every sentence, and I finally turned back to the end of Granny's. "Say your prayers every night, and trust your heavenly Father." *God? Believe in God if you like, Lucy, but He's never done anything for me except take my wife!* Oh, who was right, and how could I find out? Would that old, dull Book tell me anything I wanted to know? I would try again, for I felt torn in half, and I needed a refuge and a Counselor more than ever before, for the great question was still unsolved: who was I really going to belong to?

Today was Friday. Only two days until Sunday, and on Sunday it would come quite naturally, because everyone went to church on Sunday. On Sunday I would try again.

CHAPTER ELEVEN

A New Friend

WE SPENT MOST OF SATURDAY on the beach, swimming and playing round the boats, and in the afternoon my father walked along the coast with us to a lonely bay with white sand, where we looked for shells. I found one like a delicate pink butterfly, and I lay on the hot rocks and gazed into a pool like a miniature garden, with starfish, sea anemones, waving seaweeds, and tiny whelks. I thought that the God I had begun to seek must be a wonderful Creator to devise such fragile beauty. Tomorrow would be Sunday.

We were having breakfast in our little patio, and the bells were pealing out all over the town. "Daddy,"

I said firmly, "it's Sunday. Can I go to church like I do at home, and can I have a Bible to read?'"

"I'm afraid I haven't got a Bible," he said, "and since the churches in this town are all in Spanish, you wouldn't understand a word. Besides, they're not the kind of churches you've been used to." He hesitated, as though he had more to say, and I waited quietly, watching the patterns of sunshine through the vine leaves on the white tablecloth.

"Lucy," he said at last, "I want you to tell me this: why do you go to church? Does it mean anything to you at all, or do you just go because Granny tells you to? And do you read your Bible because it helps you or makes any difference to you? Or is it just because you've been taught that it's the right thing to do? Think it out and give me an answer. I really want to know. I dislike pious hypocrites, and I don't want you to be one."

I stared at him. Several answers sprang to my lips, but they were not real, true answers, and they would not satisfy him. He really wanted to know.

Lola and the older children had all gone to Mass in a great finery of Sunday clothes and lace, and the bells had stopped ringing. My father seemed more breathless than usual, and I hadn't the heart to ask him to come to the beach, so I sat beside him and wrote to Granny. Then I went down to the beach to look for shells by myself.

After this we were invited to dinner in the inn

kitchen, where we gathered around the table under sides of bacon and bunches of herbs and garlic hanging from the ceiling. We ate fried fish soused in tomato sauce so hot and spicy that it made my eyes water, which caused great merriment. Everyone became very cheerful and talkative. By the time we had finished (Sunday dinner started at two-thirty) it was late in the afternoon. Sunday was hurrying past, and I had still found no answer to Daddy's question nor any solution to my problem. For the first time, I felt very lonely, and my thoughts flew to the old woman up the hill. I would go and visit her.

"Daddy," I said, "I'm going to visit an old woman who lives just the other side of those eucalyptus trees. Can I take her one of our peaches?"

"Take her two, Lucy." He picked out the best and put them in a bag. "I'm glad you're making friends around here. You'll be chattering Spanish in no time, and I want you to love Spain. Don't go far, and come back before sunset."

I slipped out quietly in case the other children saw me and wanted to come with me. I liked playing with them, and I loved Rosita my *amiga,* but now I wanted to be alone. It was still very hot, and I was glad for the shade of the trees. I liked their smell, the rustle of their dry leaves, and the hum of the cicadas, who made such a noise but whom I could never see.

I walked slowly, thinking about Daddy's question. What did church really mean to me? I thought of

Sunday at home—putting on my best clothes; sniffing the cool smell of ancient stone and furniture polish; watching the sunshine making patterns through the stained-glass windows; singing the hymns as loud as I could; making up stories and poems during the sermon and hoping it wouldn't be too long; Grandpa falling asleep and Grandma looking concernedly at him out of the corner of her eye; the happy prospect of Sunday dinner, my favorite pudding, and a free afternoon. Did church mean anything more? I could not honestly say that it did, except very occasionally, as on that Good Friday morning, when I sensed some hidden beauty in a hymn or a verse of the Bible and longed for I knew not what.

When I came to the cabins at the edge of the vineyards there was no one to be seen. They were probably still all having a siesta and would come to life at sundown. So I knocked rather timidly at the old woman's door, but it was opened immediately by her gypsylike little grandaughter. I peeped in, and there was my friend sitting at the table, spectacles on nose, reading her Bible.

Why? What did it mean to her? Something, I was sure, for when she looked up at me, her face seemed transfigured, and her hands seemed to caress the book. If only I could speak to her! But since I couldn't, I did a strange, almost desperate thing. I went straight up to her and put the peaches on the table. Then I pointed to the Book and repeated the phrase that the

children at the inn said about hundred times a day—
"*¿Por qué?*" Why?

She did not seem at all surprised. She merely
pointed with a finger to a word on the page, and I
squatted down beside her to look. "*Jesús.*" It was the
same in English as it was in Spanish. She repeated it,
and then, pointing upward, she said very simply,
"*Jesús es mi Amigo.*"

Amigo. It was the word that Rosita used when we
walked down the street arm in arm and she introduced
me to all and sundry. *Mi amiga,*" because I was a girl,
but the same word. "My Friend. Jesus, my Friend."
Not someone in history, but someone near and alive,
walking beside me.

I suddenly realized as I gazed at the page that praying and churchgoing and Bible reading were no longer
three roads leading into the mist. The mist was clearing, and the roads were leading to a bright center.
They led to Jesus—not a Person in a Book who died
hundreds of years ago but Someone who was alive now.
He was the old woman's Friend, and I saw no reason at
all why He shouldn't be my Friend, too. For I suddenly knew that this was what I had been looking for
all the time—not words or rules, but a Person.

The discovery was so great that I can't quite remember what happened next. I wanted to stay near this
radiant old woman whose Friend was Jesus, but we
had exhausted our common vocabulary, and there was
no more we could say. Somehow I found myself on

the dirt track that led to the farm, and there in front
of me was the stone cross. It suddenly became terribly
important, because I remembered now that it was on
a cross that my Friend had died that I might be forgiven.

"Thank You," I said, looking up at it, and at that
moment I knew what saying my prayers really meant.
It was just talking to my Friend, saying thank you,
telling Him things and knowing that He was listening.
It was too hot to stay long near the cross, but I sat
under an olive tree and stared across at it and started
to tell Him things. I asked Him never to let me tell
lies again, and I asked Him to show me how to choose
and to make my grandparents and my father like each
other so that we could all be one family.

That special, mellow light that bathes the world before sunset already rested on land and sea, and the sun
was low above the great hills behind me. The stone
cross cast a long shadow along the path, and to my
imaginative mind the dirt track, illumined, seemed
like the beginning of a new life. I could set out on
this bright road, with all my tangled, troubled little
past behind me, and Jesus, my Friend, beside me. I
loved Him and longed for a Bible, because it no longer
seemed a dull old history book but a Book from which
I could learn about my Friend.

The sun disappeared as I came out through the
eucalyptus wood, and the sky was streaked with crimson. Lights were coming out in the shops, and the town

was waking up. My father was sitting at a table on the pavement and having a drink. I sat down beside him, happy, hot, and thirsty, and he ordered me a lemonade.

"Daddy," I said eagerly, "you know what you asked me?"

"When, Lucy?"

"This morning—about church and the Bible."

"Oh, yes? Have you thought about it?"

"Yes, and I know the answer. An old woman told me."

"What? In Spanish?"

"Yes, and I understood. I know now!"

"Really? Do tell me!"

"I want to go to church, and I want to read my Bible, because—because Jesus is my Friend."

I expected him to smile that twisty smile of his, but he didn't. He just looked at me and then replied very gently, "In that case, Lucy, I'll get hold of a Bible for you as soon as I can. And if there's such a thing hereabout, and if you're happy to go on your own, I'll find an English church service for you."

CHAPTER TWELVE

At the Tip of Spain

WAKING UP THE NEXT MORNING was a wonderful experience. At first all seemed as usual—the patch of sunlight on the wall, the lap of waves on the pebbles, the shouts of the fishermen. But then I remembered that everything was different. I was no longer a troubled child, pulled in two directions, not knowing what to believe or where to turn. I had a living, loving Friend who knew the answers and who would stay with me. I jumped up and dressed and then knelt down by my bed, and instead of gabbling off a prayer, I poured out my problem, and knew that I had been heard.

My father looked drawn and white at breakfast and

coughed a good deal. But he seemed in good spirits and suggested we take a bus down the coast to the southern tip of Spain, where I could see the Rock of Gibraltar and the north coast of Africa, and I could have a swim. I was thrilled, for I loved seeing things with my father. He was such good company and knew so much about everything. I seized my bathing suit and we went to the bus stop and bought a picnic in the market while we waited.

I shall never forget that day, and yet I had no knowledge at the time that it was a very special day, because nothing very special happened. We were just happy together. The bus rolled along the coast road with the sea on one side and the vineyards and olive groves on the other and sometimes a field of sunflowers, all facing east. My father talked about the civil war and the siege of the great castle at Toledo, where the General's son was held as ransom for the surrender of the fort. But the General did his duty. "Commit your soul to God, cry 'Long live Spain,' and die like a patriot, my son," said his father on the phone, and the fort held out until troops marched in to its rescue.

No one could tell stories like Daddy, and he held me spellbound until the rattling bus lurched round a corner and I gave a gasp; for there in front of me lay the straits, sapphire blue, and the Rock of Gibraltar like a grand, old lion couched in the sea. Across the straits, misty but visible, were the high mountains of the north African coast.

We switched from the civil war to the habits of the rock apes of Gibraltar and the snake charmers of Tangiers, and as the road wound down in hairpin bends, Gibraltar seemed to rise higher and higher into the sky. Then the bus rattled into the town and stopped near the port, where a steamboat was just arriving.

It was very, very hot down there. We ate ice cream under the red and white striped awning of a little café, where about half the customers had dark skin and spoke Arabic instead of Spanish. Then we looked in the shops at the guitars and castanets and silk-embroidered shawls, and I chose presents for my grandparents, which delighted me. I took a long, long time deciding on a tile portraying the Rock of Gibraltar for Granny's teapot and a red and gold leather spectacle case for my grandfather. My father sat on a chair in the shop, smoking and half asleep, and did not hurry me at all.

Then we sauntered along by the water's edge to the beach, a curve of white sand with palm trees shading one end. In an instant I had slipped unto my bathing suit and was speeding toward the sea, dashing into the small waves, falling headlong, and striking out toward deep water. I thought that first cool plunge was the most wonderful feeling on earth.

"Don't go too far," shouted my father, and I turned and swam back toward him. I wished he would come in too, but he usually seemed to lack energy. When at last I finished bathing, he had found a shady corner and unpacked the picnic. I flung myself down beside him and laughed aloud for the joy of sunshine, blue sea, and a strong body—and that other new joy, which I had almost forgotten because it didn't seem a separate joy any longer, just the source and light and color of all joy. But I could not have put it into words. It was just a feeling.

"Tell me more about that old woman yesterday," said my father suddenly. "She interests me."

I looked up eagerly.

"She's a nice old woman. She lives in a tiny house on the other side of the eucalyptus trees. She's got a cat and a goat and a whole basket of kittens and a little granddaughter and a Bible, and I've visited her twice."

"But how do you communicate? Surely she doesn't know English?"

"Oh no; but I told you, she's got a Bible, and we read it together. She pointed to the word 'Jesus,' and it's the same word in English and Spanish."

"I see! and what happened next?"

"She said Jesus was her *Amigo,* and I know that word, too. Rosita calls me her *amiga.* It means friend."

"A conversion unparalleled in brevity," murmured my father. "Never mind; go on. Tell me more."

I munched my sandwich thoughtfully, half turned away from him, because I suspected he was laughing at me. But when he spoke again his voice was quite serious. "Please, Lucy. I really want to hear the rest."

"Well," I began rather shyly. "I wanted Him to be my Friend too. So I went to the cross—"

"The cross? What do you mean?"

"Along the path by the vineyards. There's a farm with a little, white pig loose outside and some hens, and near the gate there's a stone cross. You know, like in the hymn; 'He died that we might be forgiven, He died to make us good.' And I sat there until I was too hot, and then I sat under a tree."

"And what did you do under the tree?"

"Well—I said I was sorry, and then, well, I said thank You. And after that, well, I asked Him to be my Friend, too."

"And what happened?"

"Well, I walked home. The cross was behind me, and everything in front was sort of shining from the sunset. And I was happy, because now I've got a Friend and I can tell Him all my troubles."

"Your troubles, Lucy? I should like to know your troubles too. What are they?"

I turned and faced him steadily. "I asked Him to make you and Granny and Grandpa like each other, so we can all be one family," I said. "That's my biggest trouble. It's horrid having to choose. Can I have a banana, please?"

He did not ask any more questions. He lay back on the sand and closed his eyes, and I thought he was asleep. Only when I got up to run back to the sea did he speak.

"The time's getting on," he said. "Run and have a last swim, and then we must get back to the port."

We boarded the bus in the cobbled square. I sensed that my father was very tired, and we traveled home almost in silence. I leaned my head against his shoulder and gazed my last on the Rock, the straits eastward, and the north African ranges southward across the sea, until the bus swung round a corner and they were gone.

My father went straight to bed when we got home, and I went into the kitchen and sat with Rosita under some dried fish hanging from a beam and ate a tortilla. There was great excitement, because Lola's brother had come from Barcelona and brought a little rubber boat that you could blow up and float on the waves. Pepito and Pedro just could not wait for next morning and would gladly have set out in the dark had they been allowed to do so. Their uncle was a large man with shiny black hair. He laughed a lot and drank a lot, and we all got very warm and merry. It was quite late when I left them still celebrating and slipped into our own apartment. The moon was shining right over the patio, and I could hear my father's rather fast breathing. I tried to tiptoe in without waking him, but he called to me.

I had kissed him good night and was leaving the room when he spoke again. "Lucy," he said, "if what that old woman told you makes you happy, hang on to it. That sort of thing cheered your mother up when she was expecting you. You may need it, one of these days."

I asked him to explain, but he said it was time to sleep. I climbed into bed and lay awake for a long time watching the moonlight on the white wall and wondering what he meant.

CHAPTER THIRTEEN

Rescue

THE NEXT DAY, Pedro and Pepito came knocking at
our apartment in a great state of excitement to say that
the stout uncle from Barcelona was taking them down
to the sea with the rubber boat. Would I like to come
too? They were taking a picnic and walking along the
beach to the little, lonely bay with the white sands,
and they were starting right now. Even Rosita was
being given a day off from her many household duties,
and Concha would ride on Uncle's back.

I hesitated. I wanted to go, but it would mean
hours away from my father. "Couldn't you come too,
Daddy?" I said.

"Not now," he replied. "I must do some work this morning. My publishers are after me. But I may stroll along and join you after lunch. There's an offshore wind today, and it's not too hot."

So we all set off in our bathing things, dancing along at the margin of the waves, and the offshore wind blew the foam lightly backward. Uncle from Barcelona was so jolly, he kept the children in fits of laughter with his jokes and stories and his imitation of a bullfight he had attended. But I could not understand, so I tripped along in front, enjoying the beach and the smells and sounds—the tarry smell of ropes, the fishy smell of nets, the salt smell of seaweed, and the sound of the screaming of gulls. I walked slowly, looking for shells and running in and out of the water and wishing this walk could last forever. But it was not so far, after all. We scrambled over the last barrier of rock, and there we were in our special bay, long before dinner time.

The rubber boat was a great success, and we all had rides in turn, with Uncle, who was not very good at swimming, splashing along behind like an enormous porpoise. Pedro and Pepito loved it and climbed in and fell out at least fifty times. Then, exhausted with swimming, laughing, and shouting, we drew the boat ashore and settled down on the sand to eat *boccadillas*—half-loaves of bread cut across and crammed high with sardines, olives, gherkins, and tomatoes—after which we ate slice after slice of watermelon. Uncle felt uncommonly thirsty. He gazed thoughtfully shoreward and indicated a gay awning in the far distance behind the sand dunes.

By his gestures I gathered that he was going to have a drink and that he would soon be back, and until he came back no one was to go into the sea or play with the boat. Rosita, Pedro, and Pepito nodded vigorously; they were good, obedient children. But Concha was not listening; she sat with her back to us, absorbed in building a sand castle, singing a happy, tuneless little song, and no one took any notice of her.

Uncle left us, and Rosita and I searched for treasures in the rock pools, while Pedro and Pepito went off to roll down the sand dunes. It was very peaceful in this small bay, and since it was lunchtime, we were the only people there. The pools were fascinating, and I lost all track of time.

Then suddenly Pedro and Pepito began screaming, loud, raucous screams that shocked the drowsy silence. Rosita and I whirled around to see them running across the sand, pointing and screaming.

Pointing at what? We turned and saw. Some way out to sea, the rubber boat bobbed on the sparkling water. In it, tranquil and as yet unalarmed, sat three-year-old Concha, enjoying the ride.

We all ran and we all screamed and we all hurled ourselves into the sea, but Rosita realized at once that we could never reach her. The boat, carried by the offshore wind, was moving out to sea much quicker than we could swim, tipping dangerously in the deeper swell. Rosita hauled in her brothers and gave frantic directions. They were to run like the wind to the café and fetch Uncle, and I was to run like the wind in the other direction to where we had seen the fishermen painting their boats and mending their nets. She would stay and watch lest Concha should feel frightened and fall into the sea.

Never before had I run as I ran that day. It was quite a distance, but I would reach the next beach before the little boys reached their uncle, for they had to climb sand dunes and find their way through the streets. I ran unseeing, blinded with horror, for it was all our fault. And how would I explain in Spanish? And would they still be there, and would they come? And if they did come? Concha was only a baby. Supposing when we got back there was just an empty boat bobbing on the waves?

"Please, please, God!" I cried, and suddenly I remembered He was not far away at all. He was the Friend close beside me who had once walked on the waves. He could still walk on the waves and reach that bobbing little boat with its precious burden. "Please, oh please," I whispered as I sped across the sand.

"My dear Lucy, are you practicing for the Olympics?"

The relief was so great that for a moment I thought my Friend had spoken out loud. Then I realized I had bumped into my father strolling along to join us. I flung my arms around his waist, too breathless to speak, looked up at him, and pointed backward.

He saw by the expression of anguish in my face that something was seriously wrong, and he shaded his eyes to look in the direction of my finger. Then he gave a violent exclamation. "Go and fetch those fishermen behind the rock, and a boat," he ordered, pushing me away from him, and he began to run as I had never dreamed he could run. I, exhausted, was left panting where I stood with no wind left, yet somehow I stumbled on and rounded the arm of rock. There were two fishermen stretched out asleep on the sand in the shade of the prow of a boat.

I sprung on them and shook them, and they jumped up, swearing fierce, Spanish oaths. But I somehow managed to convey that I was in trouble and persuaded them to come and see. They followed me at a jog around into the bay, but as soon as we came in sight of the little craft, we realized that help was no longer needed. It had already arrived.

For my father had reached the boat and was swimming slowly back, propelling it with his hand, while Concha sat smiling, enjoying her little trip. Uncle and the boys had just arrived with a great many other people, all talking, gesticulating, and raising their hands to heaven. Only Rosita stood tense and rigid, her black eyes enormous in her white face. I ran to her and took her hand, but she did not seem to notice me.

And now they were in shallow water, and my father gave the boat a little shove. It was carried in on the breaking waves, and Concha, like a dark, curly water-baby, came running in through the spray straight into Rosita's arms.

And then several things happened at once. First, Rosita had hysterics and sank down on the beach, laughing and crying and clasping her frightened little sister. Pedro and Pepito broke into bellows of relief, and the crowd closed around them, loud in their joy and emotion. Everyone pushed and jostled around the children, and no one except me turned to welcome the man walking in from the sea.

How slowly he walked! He seemed to be staring at me without seeing me, and his face was a strange, blue-gray color. I ran into the water and held out my hands, and he reached out blindly toward me and stumbled to the margin of the waves. Then he swayed and fell face downward on the sand, drawing great gasping breaths.

He was instantly surrounded by the noisy, excited crowd, and for a time I could not see what was happening. I think one of the fishermen was trying to do artificial respiration, and Uncle was running up the beach. I heard the words *policía* and *ambulancia* repeated many times, and more and more people arrived as though they had sprung up through the sand. I tried to push my way through the crowd, but I was held back, for they needed room at the center. Rosita stood weeping beside me, with Concha still clasped in her arms. Then the noise died away, and quietness seemed to gather around the still figure in the center. People began shaking their heads and sighing deeply, and every moment seemed eternity. At last we heard the siren wail of the ambulance, and some men in uniform came running down the beach, followed by two policemen in shovel hats.

They dispersed everyone in no time and carried my father away on the stretcher. I struggled loose from the restraining crowd and ran after them, pleading to be allowed to go with him. But they explained in a torrent of Spanish that this could not be. The door was slammed in my face, and my father was borne away, I knew not where.

We wandered home in a sorry procession, Uncle muttering and much put out, the boys silent and subdued. Rosita, loving and consoling, walked beside me and seemed to be trying to make me understand that nothing could possibly go wrong once the *ambulancia* and the *policía* had come in on it. But the *policía* had slammed the door in my face, and my father's face in the *ambulancia* had still looked gray. I shook my head and refused to be comforted.

When we reached the inn, the children poured out the story to Lola, who wept and scolded Concha and hugged her and scolded the family and wept more. But when she heard about my father, she dumped Concha on the bed and folded me in her arms. Then

she sent her brother, who was getting very tired of
running, quickly to the hospital to ask for news.

He was away a long time, and we sat huddled in the
low kitchen. Concha played and sang to her doll, and
Rosita could not take her eyes off her. Lola tried to
tempt me with shrimps and slices of salami, but I
could do nothing but wait with every nerve of my
body.

At last we heard fast, heavy footsteps in the street,
and Uncle came back. They all gathered around him
in the middle of the room and started talking and talking. I watched their faces and gathered from their
nodding heads and eloquent hands that my father was
still alive. Then Lola threw a shawl over her head,
held out her hand to me, and pointed up the hill, so I
supposed we were going to the hospital.

The hospital was right at the top of the town, and
we twisted our way up many sloping, cobbled streets
before we reached its iron gates. When we rang the
bell, a face peered through a grating and we were ad
mitted by an old nun. She and Lola talked rapidly in
low voices, and I sat down on a bench. The afternoon
sun was all shut out. I gazed around the large, cool
corridor that smelled of disinfectant and wondered
where my father was and what he looked like now.
Opposite me on the wall hung a crucifix—not a stone
cross like the one by the farm, but a cross with a figure
on it, and I shuddered as I looked. This was what had
happened to my Friend.

And then I suddenly remembered that the crucifixion was something that had happened nearly two thousand years ago; it was all over, and death had not been the end. My Friend had come back, and was alive and strong and able to help me. I turned my face away from the figure on the cross and thought of my father. That last desperate swim, and little Concha safe and alive and singing in the kitchen, while Daddy had nearly died instead. He had got there just in time to save her. Perhaps if I could see him and tell him, he would understand.

The nun came over to where I was sitting. She was a gentle old woman with a smooth face, and mercifully she knew a few words of English.

"The father," she said, "very ill—bad heart—come, but no much talk!" She laid her fingers on her lips, and I followed her up a staircase, her dress rustling on the stone. She opened the door into a small, private ward and glanced in. Then she took my hand and led me to the bed.

My father sat propped upright with pillows, and in his nostril he had a rubber tube attached to a cylinder. His face was still a strange color, but the loud breathing had stopped, and his eyes were open and fixed on me. I kissed him very gently and sat down as close as possible beside him. The nun waited by the door.

"Lucy, darling," my father spoke in a whisper, and his words came haltingly. "Are you all right?"

"Yes, Daddy. Are you? You're better, aren't you?"

"A little. Is Lola here?"

"Yes, she's downstairs. Shall I fetch her?"

"In a minute—stay a little longer—then I want to tell her to send a telegram to your grandfather. He must come at once."

"And when he comes, will you see him and talk to him?"

"Yes—yes. I want to talk to him. Is Concha all right?"

"Yes, quite all right. She's singing, and they're all so glad she's alive." I hesitated, not quite knowing how to say what I wanted to say so much. "Daddy, you nearly died, didn't you, so that Concha would be rescued and not drown. And Daddy, I was thinking, it was rather like Jesus on the cross, wasn't it? You know, 'He died that we might be forgiven'—because if you hadn't swum out and nearly died, she'd have been carried right away or fallen out. You got there just in time, didn't you?"

He closed his eyes, and the nun came forward and laid her hand on my shoulder.

"Little girl, come," she said. "The father very ill, so you go now. Tomorrow he better. Tomorrow come."

But she waited while I kissed him, and he held my hand in both his own and opened his eyes again.

"Yes, just in time," he whispered. "It had tilted badly, and she was slipping sideways. Wasn't it a good thing, Lucy, that I got there just in time?"

CHAPTER FOURTEEN

En Mi Corazón

THE NEXT DAY seemed very long, and I wasn't allowed to see my father until five o'clock in the evening. I was not particularly anxious about him, because he had come around, and once people started getting better, I supposed they usually went on getting better. Also the nun had said, "Tomorrow he better!" and she ought to know, if anyone did.

Besides, if it hadn't been for his illness, my prayer would never have been answered; but now all that I longed for was going to happen. Grandpa was coming—at least I was pretty sure it would be Grandpa, for he would not want Granny to come alone, and one of them would have to stay with the poultry. He and

130

my father would talk and be friends; I was quite sure of that. Everyone liked Grandpa, and Grandpa would see at once that Daddy was a good man now. How could he think otherwise when Daddy had nearly died saving Concha? And then, of course, Daddy would come back to Pheasant Cottage when he was better, and we would all be one happy family at last!

I did not know how to pass the hours as I waited for that reply telegram. Suppose it got lost, or suppose Grandpa who had never been out of England and knew no Spanish, got lost! Or suppose he had bronchitis and Granny wouldn't let him come?

Our own apartment seemed lonely and forlorn without Daddy, and I did not want to go there; I had shared Rosita's bed on the previous night. But the kitchen felt too crowded for my restless mood, and I did not feel like staying there, either, so I took Concha and Francisco for a walk along the seafront. But the stroller was so heavy in the heat, and fat Concha walked so slowly! I could understand a good deal of what the children said by now, but I longed for someone to talk to, and my thoughts flew back to the old woman. I had never been to tell her what had happened, and I knew she would be interested. I waited until siesta time, when, in summer, all sensible Spaniards go to sleep in preparation for the bright, exciting night ahead. Then I slipped out and crossed the main road into the shade of the eucalyptus trees.

As usual, the rustling fragrance of the hot wood

quieted me, and I walked slowly. If I spun out the time, perhaps on my return the telegram would have come.

I had thought the old woman might have been asleep too, but she wasn't. She was over near the olive grove pasturing her goat on the rough grass, which, growing in the shade, still bore some trace of green. I trotted along the dirt track and joined her under the trees, and her wrinkled old face lit up when she saw me, as though I was very dear to her. She started talking rapidly, and although I could not understand, I knew that it was loving, endearing talk. I looked up at her.

"*Mi padre,*" I said. "*Muy malo.*"

I had heard these words many times, on the beach, at the inn, and in the hospital, and now they had a tremendous effect. They produced a torrent of sympathy and offers of *pan* and *leche* which I knew meant bread and milk. I had felt too restless for my dinner, and it had been too oily for my liking, so now I was hungry. I smiled and nodded and slipped my hand into hers, and we wandered back to the hut, the goat skipping behind and occasionally butting me in the back in quite a friendly way.

The hut was bare and clean as before, and there was no sign of the gypsy grandchild, for which I was thankful, for I wanted to be alone with this old woman who knew my Friend. But I said nothing at first, for she was busy heating goat's milk and cutting slices from a freshly baked loaf. I ate and drank with enjoyment, looking around at the quilted bed, the worn rag mat, the milking stool, and the few kitchen utensils ranged around the stove. On an upturned box covered with a clean cloth lay the Bible, our one real point of contact.

She sat watching me as I ate, beaming at me, and I wondered why she seemed to love me so, because I was quite an ordinary looking child, and Spaniards usually had plenty of their own. But whatever the reason I felt very much at home, and as soon as I had finished eating and drinking I went over to the Bible and put my hand on it and repeated, slowly and clearly, the words she had said to me: *"Jesús es mi Amigo."*

She was delighted. She nodded her head many times, and her already smiling face became radiant. Then she pointed upward, laid her other hand over her heart, and said *"Jesús está en mi corazón."*

I stared, for once again I had understood. *Corazón* meant heart, and I had heard it at least twenty times in the last hours. Men on the beach had whispered it, laying their hands on their chests and shaking their heads. Lola had said it with tears in the bar the night before, and the old nun had said it, nodding very fast and looking wise. My father had had a heart attack. I had heard about them before. I had once asked him why he swallowed so many pills and why he walked so slowly and why he didn't come swimming, and he had told me that he had a weak heart and had to be careful. But when he had seen little Concha sailing off toward the ocean he had not been careful. And that was why he was in the hospital, and that was why Grandpa was coming. I recalled my straying thoughts and tried to think what the old woman meant.

"Jesús está en mi corazón." This seemed to describe what I had been feeling. I suddenly remembered my Bible at home, and the picture in the front of it—Jesus knocking at a door with weeds growing all over it. One day I had asked Granny what door it was and who He was trying to visit, and she had told me it was a famous picture of our Lord knocking at the door of the human heart. I had not been very interested, but now I suddenly felt that a light had shone on that picture.

"Come in," I whispered, "oh please, please come in!" And then I realized that He had been there ever since I had asked Him to be my Friend, teaching me to care more about other people, giving me this new longing to know more about God, and making me happier. He had not waited for me to put it into words; He'd just come to me as soon as I had wanted Him and cried out to Him. Perhaps wanting Him was the same as opening the door if you did not understand much or know how to say it right. I suddenly felt strong and glad and alive and wanted to run and jump in spite of the hot, drowsy afternoon, but I did not do so. I sat quietly listening while the old woman murmured on in Spanish, and though I couldn't understand a word, it all sounded very peaceful and re-assuring.

After a while I kissed her and went home, for per-haps a telegram would have arrived, and it would soon be time to visit Daddy.

The telegram had arrived. All the children were running in all directions looking for me, and Pepito spied me first and sped to meet me, black locks blown back from his forehead, black eyes sparkling. He siezed my hand and dragged me to the kitchen, where Lola produced the envelope from under her apron bodice, and they all stood round while I opened it.

"STARTING IMMEDIATELY STOP ARRIV-ING MALAGA 10:15 THURSDAY STOP GRAND-PA." I read it over and over. Tomorrow by midday, Grandpa would be here. With much talk and waving of hands, Lola gave me to understand that she had an *amigo* in Malaga who would meet him and put him on the bus, and we would all go and await his arrival in the market square.

I just could not wait to show my father the telegram. Lola had already been up to the hospital to inquire, and they had said that he was better, so I set out alone, clutching the precious paper and counting the hours. It was nearly five o'clock. Grandpa would be here by tomorrow's lunch time—about nineteen hours, and I would be asleep for about nine of them. That left ten waking hours, and I wondered how I would get through them. I climbed the cobbled streets slowly, for I knew I was early, but the kind old nun sat me in her office and gave me a picture book of Spain. The minutes ticked by until she reappeared and said, "You come now. The father he better."

He really did look a little better, although he still tired quickly if he talked much, so I talked to him instead, and showed him the telegram. I told him how lonely I was without him, and how I had slept with Rosita and had been to see the old woman and feasted on goat's milk and hot brown bread. He smiled.

"You do know how to look after yourself, don't you, Lucita?" he said. "What did you and old lady talk about this time?"

I looked down shyly.

"Tell me, Lucy. I like hearing about the old lady."

I looked up at him.

"She said, '*Jesús está en mi corazón.*' I knew what that meant, because they all talk about your *corazón*. It means 'heart,' doesn't it?"

"Well, yes. But perhaps not quite the same kind of heart."

I wanted to ask him what he meant, but he seemed rather breathless, so I described the opening of the telegram and talked about Grandpa's arrival next day. He seemed very glad at the prospect of seeing Grandpa, and when the nun came to take me away I skipped home without a care in the world, because everything was going to be all right. I ran to the beach before going to the inn and sat on a rock and watched the colors on the sea while the sun went down behind the hills. I prayed that my father's heart would get better quickly, and that he and my grandfather would become friends so we could all live happily ever after like one family. Then, quite sure that my prayer had been heard, I went in to supper and passed a pleasant evening playing with Rosita and Pepito and chewing sunflower seeds.

I slept with Rosita again, but was awakened in the middle of the night by Concha. She was having a nightmare and rising up and screaming in the large cot she shared with Francisco. She did not say anything at all, and was probably still asleep; she just screamed. But Lola was there in a moment. She did not speak, either. She gathered the trembling little girl into her arms and carried her to the safety of her own big, brass bedstead; and Concha stopped screaming at once.

Rosita had not awakened, for she was used to nightmares, but I could not go to sleep again for a time. There was so much to think about—Daddy at the hospital, Grandpa probably already in London, and my Friend in my heart. Like Concha, I had understood so little and had known no words to express what I wanted. But it hadn't mattered at all. He had heard my cry in the dark and He had come at once and taken me into the shelter and safety of His love.

CHAPTER FIFTEEN

Saying Good-bye

WE ALL ARRIVED much too early in the square to meet
the bus into which it was to be hoped that Lola's *amigo*
had shepherded Grandpa. Grandpa had never been
out of England before, and I felt that anything might
happen to him on his own in Spain.

My excitement and anxiety had infected all the rest
of the family and we hopped up and down, waved and
shouted at the wrong buses coming around the corner,
and altogether made quite an exhibition of ourselves!
We had been up since early morning, cleaning the
apartment, marketing, and cooking a special dinner.
Although I wanted us to dine all together in the
kitchen, Lola had insisted that Grandpa and I should

dine alone on the first day. It was only later that I
realized that pork chops, new potatoes, and early
grapes were far too expensive a meal for the whole
family.

And then, at last, the right bus swept around the
corner and stopped in front of us, and there was
Grandpa in his black Sunday suit and panama hat. He
was peering shortsightedly into the crowd in every
direction except the right one. I just had time to notice how very English and out of place he looked in
Spain, and then I was in his arms before he had even
seen me. Lola and the children were pressing in on us,
smiling, curtseying, and shaking hands, escorting him
down the street that led to the inn, all talking Spanish
all at once, with Grandpa, perspiring, smiling, nodding, and none the wiser!

Only when he was comfortably seated in the patio
under the vine did we really greet each other. He had
removed his hat and coat and had a wash, and Lola
had brought him a mug of chilled fruit juice. He was
feeling much better and took a good look around.

"It's very warm here, isn't it, Lucy?" he remarked.
"And I must say you are looking well, though perhaps
a little thinner. And how brown you are, my dear!
And how's your poor father?"

I sat down beside him on a cushion and talked and
talked about my poor father, his kindness, his good-
ness, his courage, and how he had nearly given his life
for Concha. And Grandpa sat watching me, his blue

eyes rather troubled and anxious, but he did not inter-
rupt me until I paused for breath.

"Your Granny, Lucy—she's quite well, but she finds
it kind of hard to settle when you're not there. She's
just counting the days until you come home."

"Well, I won't be long," I replied. "Daddy's getting
better, and it's not long now until school. Tell me
about home, Grandpa. How's the garden? And how's
Shadow?"

He chatted on, and I sat at his feet and drank in
every detail. I had not realized how much I missed
home, because there had been so much to think about.
But now it was all coming back—Granny hanging up
the washing under the apple trees (they would be
almost ripe for picking now); the good smell of English baking without oil; the mountain-ash berries beginning to redden; butterflies on the michaelmas
daisies; Shadow rolling on green, green grass; the
smell of summer rain on bracken. Spain suddenly
seemed very parched and hot. Pepito and Pedro kept
peeping through a crack in the door and being chased
away by Lola and coming back again, but I hardly
noticed them. I was back at home, waist-deep in willow
herb.

Grandpa noticed them, however. He opened his
luggage and presented them with a big bag of mixed
sweets from Woolworth's. They thanked him joyfully
with mouths, eyes, and hands, and we could hear them
for a long time exulting in the kitchen. Then Lola

came in with the dinner, and all the children came behind her carrying little dishes and bottles. I showed off my few words of Spanish, to the amazement of Grandpa, who responded to all attempts to communicate by smiling and nodding. He pecked rather doubtfully at the highly seasoned, oily food, but I ate an enormous meal and thoroughly enjoyed myself.

After lunch Grandpa had a long sleep, for he said he had not slept a wink in his noisy London hotel, and he was feeling the heat. But at five o'clock we set out and walked up to the hospital almost in silence. Grandpa was obviously nervous and kept clearing his throat and mopping his brow. I was quiet because I was approaching the great moment of my life: my conflict was about to be resolved, my prayer was about to be answered. Daddy and Grandpa were going to meet.

I hoped the old nun would not take us up to the ward, for I wanted to stage this myself, and to my relief she wasn't there. The doorkeeper let us in and nodded to the stairs. Grandpa was walking very slowly now, almost as though he were afraid, but I just could not wait. I ran ahead, slipped into the room without knocking, and took up my favorite position in the crook of my father's arm.

"He's coming, Daddy," I announced. "Grandpa's coming up the stairs now. Are you ready?"

Grandpa's head came cautiously around the door, and I wondered, for an instant, just what sort of a monster he expected to see! But at the sight of my father, so pale and weak, propped against pillows, his expression changed suddenly to one of great concern and compassion. He hurried across the room, both hands outstretched.

"Mr. Martin," he cried. "How very, very sorry I am to see you like this, sir. Lucy has been telling me about your—er—great courage in saving that child." He had clasped Daddy's free hand, and Daddy was smiling his gentle, pleased smile, not the twisty one which meant he was making fun of someone. It was all most satisfactory, and I somehow felt it was all my doing! I swelled with pride and pleasure.

"Draw up that chair, Mr. Ferguson," said my father. "I can't talk too much—get a bit breathless. But it's good to see you. Lucy, wait downstairs—I want to talk to Grandpa. Come and say good-bye later."

I trotted away and wandered around the old, walled garden fenced from the sea winds by tall cypress trees and smelling of thyme and lemon verbena. I was very happy, for everything was ending up right. Daddy and I would soon go home together, and he would get better at Pheasant Cottage, where it was cool and green, and great beeches cast shade. He would sit and write his books in the garden, and I would take him cups of coffee and post his manuscripts, and next summer we would come back to Spain to Lola and Rosita and the children and the sea and the fishing boats and the old woman.

"Lucy, your father's waiting to say good-bye."

Grandpa was standing on the steps, and I ran to him joyfully. "Did you like him, Grandpa?" I asked. "I told you he was a good man, didn't I?"

"Yes, yes, Lucy; he's a good, brave man. Go to him now, but don't stay long. He's very tired."

I obeyed, wondering. Why did Grandpa seem so distressed? And why were there tears in his eyes? Perhaps my father would tell me. I slipped into his room and hesitated: he lay so still, and his face was such a strange color.

"Lucy, darling, come here." He managed to lift his arm and put it round me. "I wish I could explain, but I've been talking too long—I'll just have to tell you— I want you to go home with Grandpa tomorrow—you can't stay here alone. I shall miss you. Hasn't it been a lovely holiday?"

My face flushed crimson, and a storm of protest rose to my lips. Leave him alone? It was impossible! I would stay with Lola and visit him every day and pack for him when he came home. But he pressed my hand.

"Lucy, darling, I'm too tired to argue," he said. "It's just got to be! Come in the morning and say good-bye. I'll explain then. And Lucy—never, never hate! What a stupid waste of time it all was. What a good old man he is!"

There was nothing more to be said. He kissed me and closed his eyes. I leaned against him for a moment or two, gulping back my tears, and then slipped away. As I came downstairs I could see Grandpa sitting on

the bench in the hall waiting for me, but he did not
hear my footsteps, for he sat deep in thought, with his
head bowed and his hands pressed between his knees.
He seemed such a sad, old man that all my arguments
and protests died on my lips, and I suddenly felt
afraid. What had gone wrong? They had met and
liked each other, and Daddy would get better and
come home. I put my hand softly on Grandpa's shoulder, and he jumped.

"Grandpa," I whispered tearfully, "couldn't I wait
until he's better? He'll need someone to carry his suitcase when he comes home. He's not allowed to carry
anything heavy."

"You must do what he says, Lucy," said Grandpa,
and his voice was so sorrowful. "He told me in his
telegram to book return seats. It's all for the best, my
dear. But he'll find it hard to say good-bye in the
morning, so you must help him by being brave and
obedient." He rose to his feet, and I slipped my hand
through his arm because he looked old and sad and
feeble, and once again I wondered what could have
gone wrong.

We walked home almost in silence, and I left him
resting in extreme lowness of spirit and went into the
kitchen to tell Lola and Rosita that I had to go home.
There was an awful finality about booked seats that
neither argument nor pleading could alter.

But I was quite unprepared for the uproar that followed my announcement. Lola clasped me in her

arms and burst into tears, Rosita wrung her hands, and the little boys bellowed in unison, while their father added to the commotion by yelling at them from the bar to stop making such a noise. So we wiped our eyes and fried potatoes and had a party, and Uncle played the guitar, Rosita danced, and we all sang. Grandpa was too tired to come, so we took his supper on a tray, and it was quite late before I got back to the apartment. He seemed to be reading a book upside down and was in no better spirits.

"Grandpa," I whispered, "what's the matter? Why are you so sad? He'll come soon, won't he? And he can come to the cottage, can't he? You did like him, didn't you Grandpa?"

"Oh yes, yes; oh dear, yes," said Grandpa much distressed. "But what a lot of time we waste, Lucy, when we won't forgive! I've been sitting here thinking. I never had much book learning, and your Granny could say it a lot better than I could, but it seems to me that every hour when we won't love and forgive is an hour of life wasted. And to think of all the years when we could have done so much for him!"

"But you can do it now, Grandpa," I insisted, "We'll all do lots for him when he comes home. And do you think, Grandpa, that when he comes we could go to the plane and meet him, me and you? Because, you know, he oughtn't to carry his suitcase himself."

But Grandpa only said, "Please God we'll do all we can for him, my dear," and went mournfully to bed.

I did the same, but not to sleep. For this was the last night I would watch the moonlight wash my white wall or hear the rhythmic break of small, summer waves on pebbles or the muffled noises of the street in front of the inn—the blaring of radios, the footsteps and the chattering, the strumming of guitars from the cafés, and the mellow songs of those who had had a drop too much. I had spent my last happy evening with Rosita and her family, and tomorrow I would pay my last visit to the hospital. I buried my face in the pillow and felt miserable, but sleep overtook me almost at once. Then I awoke to my last sundrenched Spanish morning.

There were several things I had to do before we left in the afternoon. I had to pack and visit my father and say good-bye to the old woman and have a farewell dinner with the family. Mercifully, I had awakened early—they were still pulling in the nets—and I could pack my treasures before breakfast—the presents for my grandparents; Rosita's photograph; the shells I had picked up; the blue baubles from the eucalyptus trees, which I was going to make into necklaces; and the postcards I had bought of Spain and Gibraltar. I wished I had presents for the children, but I had no money, and with my father so ill it had not occurred to me to ask for any. Perhaps I could send something from England. Then I went with Rosita to fetch bread for the last time, but we kept wiping our eyes and sniffing, so it wasn't a very cheerful expedition.

My grandfather seemed to understand that I was in a great hurry, and he let me bolt my breakfast and go. We had special permission from the hospital to visit my father in the morning, I first and Grandpa later. But I did not hurry on my way there; I walked slowly, for I dreaded leaving him. But I knew it was too late to change anything, and the best way to help him was to obey as cheefully as possible.

He had just had his morning wash and shave, and he looked fresher and brighter than he had in the evening. The room faced east and was full of sunshine, and a pleasant-looking, young nun was bringing him a drink. My heart felt a little less heavy as I drew up the chair and leaned against the pillows.

"Daddy," I began, "I do wish I didn't have to leave you. Who'll visit you and look after you after I go?"

"Lola will visit me," he replied, "and I couldn't be better looked after anywhere. These nuns are wonderful. And as for that old one who comes in the afternoon—she's right up your street! She tells me she goes to the chapel and prays for me every day."

I turned to see whether he was laughing, but his expression was quite serious and rather sad.

"That's two of us then, Daddy," I said, "because I do, too."

"Then keep right on, Lucita," he said gently, and we were silent for a few moments. He seemed tired with talking, so I talked instead. I told him all my wonderful plans for when he came, and I described the summerhouse where he could sit and write, with the clematis and honeysuckle climbing in at the window. I told him about the robin who flew in and out of the spare bedroom which would be his. Grandpa had said so.

"So you see, they are longing for you to come," I finished. "You won't be long, will you?"

"I would love to come," he said, "only I can't be quite sure when. But remember, whatever happens in the future, nothing can ever take away this holiday. It's been the happiest time for me since your mother died. You've been such a perfect little companion, Lucy. It was like having her all over again. She didn't seem much older than you when I married her—and so like!"

"It's been a lovely holiday," I whispered, because my lips were trembling. "But—but—it's been rather a sad ending, hasn't it!"

He held me as close as he could.

"Not really," he said. "In fact, I sometimes think it's the happiest ending possible. You see, I've often felt sad about those years when we could have been together—and all my own stupid fault. So I'm glad I could give another little girl back to her parents. I often wake in the night and feel so thankful I got there just in time. And if I hadn't been ill I'd never have known your Grandfather. It all came right, Lucy; such a happy ending!"

He was breathless with too much talking, and the

young nun, who had been hovering outside, came over and put one hand gently on my shoulder and the other on my father's wrist. I gave him a last kiss, and she led me away, but at the door I turned and smiled through my tears.

"It was a lovely holiday," I said in a voice that only trembled slightly. "Thank you Daddy, thank you so much!"

"And thank you, too, Lucy; thank you so, so much!" he whispered, and then the door was closed softly behind me.

I had said good-bye. Everything inside me seemed too big for me. There was a tightness in my throat and chest and behind my eyes, and I did not want to go straight back to the house. Why, oh why, did I have to leave him, just when he needed me so much to visit him and to fetch things and to pack his suitcase when he got better? Almost without knowing it, my feet had been carrying me across the marketplace toward the vineyards and the olive trees. Each time I had gone there I had found comfort, and now I needed it more than ever before.

The grape harvest had begun and my old woman was working hard among the vines, her little granddaughter beside her. There were other people there, too, and they stared curiously at me as I slipped toward her through the bushes. When she saw me, she threw up her hands in delight and pressed a grape into my mouth. Then she looked at me more closely and knew that I was in trouble. She squatted on the warm soil by her loaded basket and drew me down beside her. The vines made a private shelter around us, and I tried to tell her my sorrow. My father, I explained, with much waving of hands and pointing, was still in the hospital. I, with much pointing skyward, was going to England in an *avión,* the Spanish word for *plane* much overworked by Pedro and Pepito. I had come to say *adiós.* My eyes filled with tears again.

She understood at once and murmured her sympathy, caressing my hands. Out of many incomprehensible words, there were some that I understood "Jesus . . . with me . . . Jesus . . . with you . . . Jesus . . . with your father."

"With me—with you." Concha said that all day long. "Play with me. I want to play with you." Of course I understood, and I was comforted. In my sadness I had forgotten. I was not leaving my father alone; I was leaving him with Jesus, my Friend, who loved him very much and who, so far, had made everything come right and had answered my prayers. He would be there in the quiet ward, and even if my father did not know much about Him, He knew all about my father. And the old nun was praying for Daddy, and I was, too, and my grandfather liked him. All was well.

I picked two vine leaves to press in memory of that moment, kissed the old woman, and left her lamenting and calling down heaven's blessings on my head.

At least that was what it sounded and looked like. Then as I walked back with the load of my sadness partly lightened, I remembered something else—something that made me draw in my breath, clap my hands softly, and dance down the dirt track. I was going home to Granny and Shadow!

CHAPTER SIXTEEN

Safe Home at Last

WHEN AT LAST THE LETTER CAME, I think I was almost expecting it. Nobody had told me; we had simply stopped talking about Daddy's coming home.

But before that, several things had happened. As soon as we got home, Grandpa told our vicar about my father, and he immediately got in touch with an English chaplain in the south of Spain who held services for visitors all through the summer. He started to visit my father and send us news. And it was on a day that we had received a letter from him that Granny dropped her bombshell.

We were sitting at the window table eating our lunch on that ordinary September day, when Granny suddenly put down her knife and fork and said, "It's no use, Herbert! I just can't stand it any longer!"

"Stand what, my dear Elsie?" said Grandpa, rising to his feet in alarm. "Is there something wrong with the steak and kidney?"

"Certainly not," said Granny, "I made it myself. It's just that I can no longer stand the thought of that poor, brave husband of Alice's left to the mercy of a lot of foreigners. If we sold the antique cabinet, I could go and put things to rights."

"My dear," said Grandpa, very flustered, "if you feel like that, you must go. But not the antique cabinet, Elsie; that's been in your family for hundreds of years. I could sell some of the hens. They are a valuable breed."

"Nonsense, Herbert," replied Granny. "I believe you'd as soon get rid of Lucy as get rid of those hens! The cabinet was to have been left to Lucy, but no doubt she'd rather see her father properly cared for. No, child, it's no use looking at me like that, because you are not coming with me! School starts in a week's time, and you must help take care of your Grandpa. Oh yes, Herbert, I know you're very domesticated and all that, but you'll never remember to take your cough mixture unless someone reminds you. It's not that I want to leave you, but when I think of that poor, dear man stranded in that outlandish place, where nobody speaks a word of English, I could almost cry!"

She sniffed and almost did cry. I stared at her in amazement. No one had wanted to cry or called him a poor, dear man when he was in prison—perhaps because everyone spoke English in prison. But there was no doubt about it, something had happened. In short, we had become a family.

Granny was a woman of action. She visited the vicar that very afternoon. He phoned the English chaplain, who promised to meet her and find suitable lodgings. And four days later Granny set off clad in her Sunday costume with her best tweed coat over her arm. She said that chaplains' wives abroad were always well dressed, and she would not believe how hot it was. Grandpa took her to the London airport, and I stayed the night with Mary Blossom.

I was very glad to see Grandpa back, and we settled down to look after each other in a peaceful sort of way, although he almost lived from one letter to the next. Granny wrote nearly every day and seemed to be enjoying herself. She was actually staying with the English chaplain, and his wife wasn't particularly well dressed; she mostly wore overalls. Her daughter and grandchildren were staying with her, and Granny seemed to have become part-time nurse to the baby. She went to the hospital twice a day, where she read aloud to my father and took down messages for me.

"But why can't he read himself, Grandpa?" I asked. "And why can't he write to me himself yet?"

"I don't imagine he's strong enough," said Grandpa

looking distressed. And I think it was after that that we stopped talking about Daddy's coming home.

I missed Granny a lot, but it was very restful living with Grandpa. And although the days were outwardly uneventful, for me they were days of great discovery. On first arriving home I had hugged Granny and Shadow and then run upstairs to my room to see if my Bible was where I had left it, and it was. I had been too excited and sleepy that night to open it, and next morning I had overslept, and there was so much to do and see that first day that I only peeped at it.

But on Sunday I had gone to church with my grandparents, and church seemed different—no longer an old building where I had to go on Sunday, but my Friend's house, where I could talk to Him, using those great words that others had used for centuries past as steps to God. "I believe in God the Father," I affirmed so loudly and joyfully that one or two people glanced around and smiled, and Granny looked rather anxious, because she didn't like my being peculiar. But I didn't care, for the words seemed to be singing themselves. "I believe in the Holy Ghost, the Lord the Giver of life."

Life! I had been so near to death that the very word was precious. Concha, tipping on the slippery rubber dinghy, but she was alive. My father, lying so still and gray-faced on the beach, but he had lived. And the figure on the crucifix at the hospital, but He rose again.

After dinner I went to my favorite seat on the rockery behind a screen of hollyhocks and started to read the gospel of John. "In him was life. . . ." I read very slowly on into the third chapter, "For God so loved the world, that he gave his only begotten Son, that whosoever believeth in him should not perish, but have everlasting life."

I looked around. Everything was dying, but it didn't seem important, because everywhere there were signs of new life. The petals had fallen, but the rose-hips were swelling. The butterflies on the michaelmas daisies had once been caterpillars, but each one had rolled into a chrysalis and had died; but the life had persisted. It had come bursting out of the chrysalis as a bright red admiral or tortoiseshell whose wings bore it sunward. "In him was life," and as I read I understood, although at the time I could not possibly have put it into words. My Friend was not only Jesus, who had lived on earth and healed the sick and been kind to children. He was God, and the everlasting life He had given me was His own life—the life that had created the world and breathed in the spring and quickened the earth. If I believed, I was part of it all, and part of Him. Then I thought of Daddy and wished that he could believe, too.

A week after Granny left, I went back to school and enjoyed astonishing my friends with my stories of planes and the south of Spain, Gibraltar and the Mediterranean. I even spoke a little Spanish to them and made quite a sensation. I did not say much about my father, but if anyone had asked me why, I could not have told them.

I was very busy helping Grandpa in the house and doing my homework, and had little time for reading. But I tried to read a little of John's gospel every day. I had got up to chapter 11, and on that Saturday, two weeks after the beginning of term, Shadow and I went to the woods to pick blackberries, my Testament in my pocket. It was the first of October, and I was pleasantly excited, for I knew Don would be home for the weekend. He had been away when I returned, and I had not seen him since my holiday.

I picked what blackberries I needed and then sat on a fallen tree trunk and read John 11. It was all there again, death and life: "I am the resurrection, and the life: he that believeth in me, though he were dead, yet shall he live: and whosoever liveth and believeth in me shall never die." And I knew it didn't just mean that Lazarus came back; it was His own eternal life, so that those who believed never really died at all. The seeds fell, the leaves lay buried, but the spring always came again. I put my Testament back in my pocket and went home, thinking about the apple and blackberry pie I would make for supper.

"Grandpa," I called at the front door, "where are you? I'll get dinner."

There was no answer. I glanced into the living room, and there he was sitting at the table, his face buried in his hands, an open letter in front of him. I stopped short.

"Grandpa," I cried, "what's the matter?" Shadow, sensing trouble, trotted forward and laid his nose on Grandpa's knee.

Grandpa looked up quickly, and his eyes were filled with tears. Then I knew, and realized that I had known deep down ever since Granny had gone away. This was what I had really been waiting for, and this was why life and death had seemed so important.

"My dear, dear Lucy," said Grandpa, "I don't know how to tell you—"

"It's Daddy, isn't it?" I whispered, for my throat felt rather dry. "He's dead, isn't he?" Then I ran into Grandpa's arms, and we cried together, and Shadow licked us frantically in turn.

"He passed away on Wednesday," said Grandpa, at last, "but Granny didn't telegraph, because he wanted you to have this letter as soon as you knew. He knew he couldn't last long. That was why he wanted you to leave. He wanted you safe and settled at home when you got the news. He wrote this letter just a little at a time on the days when he felt better. Would you like to read it here with me, my dear, or would you like to take it away by yourself?"

"I think I'd like to read it alone," I said, drying my eyes on Grandpa's handkerchief. "Do you mind if I go back into the wood for a bit?"

"Not at all, dearie. Just come and have your lunch when you're ready," said Grandpa. So I clutched my letter and went out, and Shadow, unsure of whom he was supposed to be comforting, rushed after me and rushed back to Grandpa several times before he decided that my need was the greater. He trotted quietly beside me, his nose against my hand.

I could hardly bring myself to open the letter, because it seemed so strange to be reading a letter from someone who had died. I went back to my tree trunk and looked around me. Autumn had come early that year, and the trees, sunkissed, were glorious in their dying. The beeches and silver birches were pale gold, and the horse chestnut tree a vivid yellow. Acorns and shining horse chestnuts lay among the leaf drifts, seeds of life awaiting their resurrection.

I drew a deep breath and opened my letter. It was quite long. He had written it on different days, a little at a time when he felt better, and in rather shaky handwriting. He told me how much he loved me, and how sorry he was about the years together we had missed. He spoke of Granny, how good she had been, how thankful he was that we had all got to know each other, how glad to leave me in such good care. I read very slowly, for the letter was nearly finished now, and he had not told me what I so wanted to know.

I drew another deep breath and read the last paragraph.

Don't be sad, Lucita. It's the best, happiest ending. I want to tell you that I know now that we shall see each other again—you, me, your mother. *He* came just in time. The chaplain was a help, but it was you who first showed me. On the beach that day. It's like you said—the cross is behind, and it's all bright in front. . . .

The writing trailed off as though he had been too tired to finish, and there was no signature. He had probably meant to go on, but he had written all I wanted to know. A robin on a mountain ash tree suddenly trilled for joy, and I looked up, through my tears, at the blurred gold and crimson and the prismed sunlight. Daddy was right; it was all bright in front. He had passed through death into some springtime of life beyond, and for me. too, nothing would ever be the same again. Daddy had opened up to me a whole new world of poetry and beauty; I had seen the sea; I had learned to love Spain and Lola and Rosita, and one day I would go back. And best of all, I had found out the real secret of eternal life—in Jesus there was life, now and forever.

Shadow suddenly barked. I brushed away my tears and looked up again. Don was racing through the wood on his way to the cottage, a living, bounding creature leaping over the crimson brambles. He turned his head and saw me.

"Hurrah, Lucy," he shouted, "all safe home at last!" and came careening toward me across the beechnuts.